AVID
READER
PRESS

MURDER BIMBO

a novel

REBECCA NOVACK

AVID READER PRESS

New York Amsterdam/Antwerp London

Toronto Sydney/Melbourne New Delhi

AVID READER PRESS
An Imprint of Simon & Schuster, LLC
1230 Avenue of the Americas
New York, NY 10020

For more than 100 years, Simon & Schuster has championed authors and the stories they create. By respecting the copyright of an author's intellectual property, you enable Simon & Schuster and the author to continue publishing exceptional books for years to come. We thank you for supporting the author's copyright by purchasing an authorized edition of this book.

No amount of this book may be reproduced or stored in any format, nor may it be uploaded to any website, database, language-learning model, or other repository, retrieval, or artificial intelligence system without express permission. All rights reserved. Inquiries may be directed to Simon & Schuster, 1230 Avenuc of the Americas, New York, NY 10020 or permissions@simonandschuster.com.

This book is a work of fiction. Any references to historical events, real people, or real places are used fictitiously. Other names, characters, places, and events are products of the author's imagination, and any resemblance to actual events or places or persons, living or dead, is entirely coincidental.

Copyright © 2026 by Rebecca Novack

All rights reserved, including the right to reproduce this book or portions thereof in any form whatsoever. For information, address Avid Reader Press Subsidiary Rights Department, 1230 Avenue of the Americas, New York, NY 10020.

First Avid Reader Press hardcover edition February 2026

AVID READER PRESS and colophon are trademarks of Simon & Schuster, LLC

Simon & Schuster strongly believes in freedom of expression and stands against censorship in all its forms. For more information, visit BooksBelong.com.

For information about special discounts for bulk purchases, please contact Simon & Schuster Special Sales at 1-866-506-1949 or business@simonandschuster.com.

The Simon & Schuster Speakers Bureau can bring authors to your live event. For more information or to book an event, contact the Simon & Schuster Speakers Bureau at 1-866-248-3049 or visit our website at www.simonspeakers.com.

Interior design by Wendy Blum

Manufactured in the United States of America

1 3 5 7 9 10 8 6 4 2

Library of Congress Control Number: 2025946611

ISBN 978-1-6682-1461-9
ISBN 978-1-6682-2891-3 (Int Exp)
ISBN 978-1-6682-1463-3 (ebook)

Let's stay in touch! Scan here to get book recommendations, exclusive offers, and more delivered to your inbox.

In memory of Amber Hollibaugh, Beth Freeman,
Cecilia Gentili, and Dorothy Allison

MURDER BIMBO

PROLOGUE

FEAR FLUNG me out of New York City. That helped. Metropolitan gravity can be a bitch. I follow the Hudson past the Bronx and hit the interstate. When my adrenaline-induced myopia clears, the city is a receding cluster of lights. Soon trees hide the lights, hills hide the trees. I pass as many cars as I can without getting pulled over.

At night the drive is seven hours. I barely make it two before I start losing it. My eyelids get heavy. My thoughts warp into dream and back. To stay awake I picture a faceless driver in a black sedan aiming a gun at me and shooting me dead. The bullet pierces his window, then mine, a needle through two layers of fabric. When that stops working, I add an imaginary fleet of police cars cresting the hill behind me.

I cross state lines. I switch highways. Eventually my exhaustion outpaces my imagination, and my head shoots up as I'm rumbling over the white line onto the shoulder. I swerve hard into the middle of the road and stop. The streetlights are gone. The sky is a canopy of stars. The air smells like toads. At some point I have entered forest, and the trees are so tightly packed on either side, it feels like I'm in a canyon.

Considering how likely it already is that I will die in the next forty-eight hours, I sure as fuck don't need to be in a car crash of my own making. I get out. I take a few laps around the vehicle, coax blood into every extremity, tell myself the blood is full of energy, wish it were cold out, cold enough to hurt me. Then I get back in the car and drive.

I promise myself when I get where I am going I can take a nap, even though there won't be time. Even if the trip takes less than seven hours, I will need to get to work. When I came up with this idea, how did I forget about the limitations of the human body? I laugh. I laugh hard enough to keep me awake for a while. Then I try other things. I bite my cheeks, my lips, my tongue; I press my nails into my palms. I shake my head so hard I get a headache.

Then I arrive. It is five a.m. Exactly to plan. *I'm doing it,* I think, *I am getting it done.* I push open the car door and swing my feet onto hairy grass. The mountain air hits my face and it still isn't cold, but there is a breeze, and in it I feel beautiful and hyper-articulate. I turn to get my bags and catch my own face reflected in the dark car window. I stop to admire my beautiful, hyper-articulate self. I look for any vestige of exhaustion, but something has washed it from me. My face is smooth and so are my movements. I look sharp and energetic. I look younger. I look alive.

I am a fucking genius, a gorgeous fucking genius, and the only thing left to do is sit down and write.

ACT I

From: Murder Bimbo
To: Justice Bimbo
October 18 at 6:25AM

Dear Justice Bimbo,

I saw you yesterday. We were on the same block in SoHo. I was walking uptown. You were passing a poster of your own enlarged face in the window of a public radio building. I probably wouldn't have recognized you if I hadn't seen your face two ways: big and flat, then small and in real life. There was something funny about the combination. I looked away then back, away then back.

"Justice for Bimbos" the poster said in big pink script across your headshot. The name of your podcast.

I had to be in Midtown in an hour and had decided to walk to burn off nervous energy, and because I don't know the subways and was a little afraid of getting lost or having to dive off the train at my stop in an embarrassing way. I didn't stop walking, but I slowed down enough to see you drop your phone in your back pocket and open the door. Then I googled you.

I was glad to have something to do while I walked. I found your podcast. I skimmed the episode titles and realized I knew your work. Or, not knew, but it seemed familiar. I had seen articles about you. Friends, people I trust, had selected episodes to convince me of your brilliance: JonBenét Ramsey, Monica Lewinsky, Aileen Wuornos. The truth is, I had never managed to click play. It's not personal. I'm just not into podcasts.

I read the short bio on your site, I found the headshot from your poster. I read a list of all your work then I read the list of your awards. I read the controversy section of your Wikipedia page which described the series you did on ultra-right-wing political candidate Meat Neck's mistress, and how the media hated her for the wrong reasons. I downloaded the first episode of the series for later.

Sorry. This probably isn't very alluring, is it: a fan letter from someone who doesn't know your work. I wish I had time to listen or at least to do a better job at lying, but I don't. And maybe that would seem creepy anyway. I can't risk creeping you out. I should get to the point.

I'm in trouble. In the fifteen hours since I passed you on the street, I've become one of your endangered women. Like with all of them, it would be hard to step back and look at me without thinking that I brought the danger on myself. I am not entirely innocent. At least I should have known better. That's the world we live in, right? You can either make every effort to be and appear innocent, if you're a woman, and usually still get fucked and blamed for it. Or you can live your life, hope the happiness outweighs the danger, and sort the rest out when you have to.

I guess now I have to.

I'm not in the city anymore. I'm in a shabby little cabin that used to be part of a kids' camp and is now used in the summer for very bare-bones corporate retreats. But it's the offseason. The water is off. The electricity is off. There are six cots pushed against the wall and I'm at the one the farthest from the door, hoping the sun will come up soon, so that the light of my computer screen doesn't act like a spotlight on my face for anyone who could be looking in the window.

Someone is coming for me.

Do you believe in fate? I definitely don't—except for when it happens to me, and then I believe in it silently, so as not to scare it away.

I saw you, I saw your photo, I looked you up. I kept walking. I thought we were just two women on our way to work. I thought your work probably included a microphone and being smart. I thought the only difference between us is that you are famous and I am not.

Then I remembered that I was about to be famous, too, in a way. Do famous people just write to each other like this?

I'm stalling. I'm nervous. There's a lot riding on this and there's no way to explain except by explaining. It's actually because of the fame that I need your help. Here goes nothing.

By now I'm sure you've heard about the assassination of Meat Neck?

I killed him.

Sincerely,

Murder Bimbo

From: Murder Bimbo
To: Justice Bimbo
October 18 at 6:36AM

Dear Justice,

I wasn't supposed to have had to flee. I wasn't supposed to be here.

In an alternate reality, you and I both did our jobs yesterday, went back to wherever we were spending the night, took showers. I slept in and got room service and listened to your podcast on my ride home. I thought, *Wow, it's so cool that I saw this person in real life and now I'm listening to her show. Wow, I actually* do *like podcasts, as long as they're really good.* I probably would have learned something.

I don't know how your night went, but mine went wrong. When the people who are after me get here, they'll arrest me and put me on trial, or they'll disappear me to some black site. Or they won't bother with any of that and they'll just kill me.

My body is so overwhelmed by continuous adrenaline rushes that the sound of my own footsteps makes me nervous. I am trying to talk myself into relaxing. Do deep breaths ever help? If I can actually calm down, I'm afraid I'll fall asleep. Then I'll really be screwed. I'm writing with my body tucked into the corner of a musty cabin, wishing I had a blanket and a hot cup of coffee.

How long do I actually have? It's minutes if they followed me. An hour if they called for backup first. Maybe half a day if they have a tracker on me and are waiting for me to stop moving before they close in. I got rid of my clothes and everything else I had, so this seems unlikely, but not impossible. My phone is a burner, the car isn't mine. What else have I missed? I'm doing my best to buy time, but I learned everything from TV and I don't even watch that much.

Based on how many of the "bimbos" on your show are dead or long out-of-the-news, I'm guessing you don't cover people at their request. I'm hoping that's only because you haven't been offered the right opportunity yet. Your podcast is dedicated to setting the story straight, resuscitating the reputations of the over-blamed and the underestimated. I'm a thirty-two-year-old sex worker who just killed a politician on what I thought were the orders of the American government. Here's your chance to catch me *before* I become a scapegoat, a punching bag, or a monster who needs reputation restitution. Please, please, please turn me into a feminist antihero.

At least hear me out. This is going to be stream of consciousness and, I hope, not a total mess. But it's the first time I'm putting the whole story together (not to mention the most I've written since I dropped out of college over a decade ago), so you'll have to forgive me if I leave big gaps or say too much in the wrong places. I'll try not to get distracted.

It started last spring with a flyer. Normal day. No sign whatsoever that I was about to be recruited into a historic assassination plot. I was on my way into Boston to meet a new client when my phone buzzed.

Last min meeting need to resched. Sry.

I was annoyed, but I was also relieved, like anyone is when they get canceled on.

I put my phone in my bag without responding and hopped off the T at the next stop. It was a chilly day but still warmer than it had been in months. It felt like spring had arrived. Strangers were smiling at each other on their way to work because it was sunny out and we had all just survived another miserable Boston winter. Crocuses were peeking through the mulch. I was into it. I needed a boost, too. Work had been rough lately. My favorite regulars' self-enforced New Year's spending diets were lasting a long time this year. Plus, that morning's client wasn't the first new client to cancel on me at short notice recently. It was either shitty luck or a cultural shift or maybe my star was falling. And there wasn't enough going on in my personal world to balance it out. Life was stagnant.

But still, there was something hopeful about that day. Maybe it was the camaraderie with strangers or the bursts of green, or that my birthday was right around the corner. Maybe it was that I loved my outfit and now instead of wasting it on a client, I was going to wear it wherever I wanted. Whatever it was, the world felt very full of potential.

I have been a sex worker for ten years. That's long enough to know (1) not to put a lot of effort into chasing guys who cancel on you; (2) not to take it personally; (3) there's probably no "last min meeting"; and (4) to enjoy the guilt-free day off when it falls in your lap.

I floated into a bookshop/café for a little treat. I considered buying a new journal, I ordered a coffee, I watched grad students opening books next to computers. I enjoyed the anonymous hum. While I was waiting for my coffee, I read all the local flyers: "FOUND CAT: KERMIT (STRANGE MEOW)," "Guitar and Piano lessons for kids," "birth/miscarriage/abortion doulas, no postpartum, ask about sliding scale." Normal stuff. Then I saw an event:

"*Women in the Clandestine Services: From OSS to NSA*"—a reading followed by an interview with a local author. It started in less than an hour.

Clandestine services had never especially interested me, but I'm as susceptible as the next guy to well-researched government conspiracies, cover-ups, assassinations, coups that look like boating accidents. Plus, I loved going to events at MIT or Harvard, because they have them in giant old rooms where you can easily imagine a couple hundred years of patriarchs determining the fates of the rest of us.

"You should go," someone said.

He was a slender man, glasses, carrying a box of books. There had been an older woman also looking at the flyer, but he had waited for her to leave. I should say, for context, that I am of "average weight" and I was wearing a dress. I am also conventionally attractive. I am not shockingly beautiful, but I know that I'm of a very approachable level of beauty. I am probably the most beautiful person most men feel able to easily address.

I clocked a name tag. The man was a bookstore cashier. I wondered if he was the kind of person who was already telling himself the story of *the day we met* as if in the distant future. Or he was an alt fuckboy. Most of the time I prefer the latter. Though, to be clear, I absolutely would never date a man for free.

"Sure," I said. We introduced ourselves.

"The author is my mom," he said.

A third possibility: He was filling out the crowd. I wasn't insulted by that. If anything, I was *more* excited, because it seemed totally plausible that the speaker was a spy and that arriving with the speaker's son would give me a better chance to meet her. The fact that the clandestine services suddenly felt like a possibility, albeit a distant one, made it seem enticing. I'm saying this was the state I was in. I was *primed* for my life to change. I wouldn't say I've always felt destined for bigger things. But if you told me my life was going to take a dramatic shift and I would become an important historical figure, I wouldn't have been surprised. Maybe that's hubris or maybe I just know myself.

My phone buzzed again. The client.

Please confirm?

I didn't reply.

"Let me help carry that box," I said. *His mom saw me carrying her books,* I imagined myself saying far in the future, *and she assumed we were friends and invited me to the post-event private dinner.* I would charm her just by being myself. She would invite me out for a drink because I reminded her of her younger self, or the young self of her long-dead best colleague/friend. My next chapter would begin. Either that, or me and the guy's mom would fuck, and that would be a pretty fun addition to the chapter I was already in.

I walked to the reading with the guy. It was half a block away and across the street in the amphitheater of a red stone building. He did not make a move. The mom did not invite me to dinner with a plan to recruit me. The mom thanked me for bringing over the box. The guy took a seat with friends. I found a spot in an empty row toward the back where a man sat next to me. He reeked in an overpowering, almost chemical way, and rather than talk to him, I found an old grocery list in my bag and folded it into a clean square, so I could take notes.

I promise this is relevant: I took three years of high school Japanese. Whatever I learned is gone now, but back then, I had integrated some of the characters into my note-taking system, because it was both impressive and private, and I still use the same system today. I dated the paper in Japanese.

"What's that?" the man next to me asked.

I knew what he was talking about. I half regretted being impressive because he already seemed like a sticky character.

"Japanese," I said. I felt my phone buzz.

Not sure if messages are going through,
need to reschedule, so sorry,
please confirm when you get this.

I did not confirm. The client had no doubt slept in the hotel room the night before or stayed up fretting all night—and now he wanted to take a nap, but needed to know I wasn't going to show up and interrupt him. Well, fuck that. He could have canceled last night or before I had woken up earlier, or before I had gotten dressed and halfway to his hotel. Don't get me started on how older white guys can't be inconvenienced at all, but if they inconvenience someone else, you better not complain because "kids these days don't want to work." He could suffer a little.

"You speak Japanese?"

"A little," I said. My phone buzzed again.

"Impressive," he said.

"Not really," I said.

"Do you speak other languages?"

"Not really."

"None?" My phone buzzed twice this time. I pulled it out of my pocket. Eight new messages from the client. I turned the phone off.

"A little Italian and a little German," I said.

His forehead lifted. I say that because I realized with that gesture that he didn't have any eyebrows. There was hair on his head. He definitely had eyelashes. It was funny that a lack of eyebrows could send me on a hair inventory. He might even have been handsome if it hadn't been for the odor.

The smell could have been agricultural, I thought. Some foods can smell like chemicals if you have enough of them. Onions? Garlic? Onions.

Besides the smell, he seemed like a normal guy. He wore jeans, running shoes, and an unzipped navy bomber, an army-green pec-skimming T-shirt. He was a few years older than me.

"You go to school here?" **Onions** said.

I forgot whether we were at MIT or Harvard.

"No," I said, "I'm too old."

"That surprises me," he said. "I would have guessed you were twenty-one."

When a man who can clearly see you're over thirty tells you that you're not only significantly younger but also of drinking age, that's stage directions, not small talk. He means "You are absolutely as innocent and fresh as you can be for someone who I can legally intoxicate." In a few years, he'll be looking for college freshmen to call "old souls."

"Thanks, I'm twenty-three," I said.

Or he may also have been a normal guy calling me youthful as a compliment. Whatever. Somewhere along the way, I had apparently gotten curious.

But he didn't keep talking; instead he texted someone. I scribbled out a few more words. He stood up and moved to another row beside another woman, also "about twenty-one." I considered calling out to her to protect herself. But he didn't talk to her. Then the lecture started and for forty minutes I tried very hard to keep my mind on women in the clandestine services.

I was more tired than I knew and the HVAC hum didn't help. Several times I found myself daydreaming about going home with the author, taking off her clothes, her fucking me.

When she stopped talking the host came up for the Q&A portion.

I jerked my head up. Had I actually fallen asleep-asleep? I wanted to stand and shake out my legs. Just as I was identifying the least intrusive way out of the lecture hall, applause began. I stood to go and the other women in my row followed my lead and stood to clap. Then everyone was standing. Onions looked at me like I was a little crazy for starting a standing ovation at an MIT or Harvard reading. I shrugged, smiled, considered sitting back down, but left instead.

After the reading I kept my phone off and enjoyed that unique high of walking around knowing no one can find you and no one can reach you. If you miss something important with your phone off, it's not your fault. It's a free pass on not caring about the latest doom for a while.

The lecturer had started out as a visual analyst, back before women were very common in clandestine service agencies. When she started, she had been siloed away from the main offices with a team of near retirees who hazed her (left porn around), before training her to decipher blurry aerial images. Her job was to look at photographs of the same place taken at regular intervals over long periods of time. The shapes would change or move. Her job was to put together a story about what was happening. Trucks moved materials in and weapons out. A hole was dug. A factory got abandoned. She did not tell us where the photos were from. That was still classified. She said it wasn't boring, it was just "a subtle kind of interesting." Sounded pretty boring to me.

But those were the old days, she said. Women could do way more jobs now. She told us about the last job she had before retiring, posing as the housekeeper of a criminal's girlfriend, and how no one expected it when she was the one to separate the guy from his security so someone could arrest him. "No one expects a mom-looking person, they just think you're there to clean something," she said.

She had other stories, too, more exciting ones, with travel. Someone asked her how many different people she'd pretended to be over the years and she said probably dozens, but they weren't easy to keep straight, because they were all based on a few archetypes. Someone asked if she'd ever shot someone and she said "No comment." Someone asked how many languages she spoke, and she said eight, but that that was because she was a nerd, and not because it was required. Someone asked if she'd driven a tank or a motorcycle or a snowmobile or a McLaren or a Jet Ski and she said *no, yes, no, yes, once on Lake Powell as a teenager*. Someone asked her if she'd ever dyed her hair, and someone else interrupted on her behalf to say that was a dumb question, which was too bad because I really wanted to know. She never got back to it.

She said the most important qualities for someone to succeed in the clandestine services are curiosity, open-mindedness, and courage. Maybe former agents are taught to talk like that, to make everyone feel like they could do the job, but I really did feel like I would have been good at everything she'd mentioned. I wasn't sure I could handle years of blurry photos in "Wherever, Virginia," but the years when she was a case officer abroad sounded—well, pretty fun.

I got back to my neighborhood around five refreshed. I thought maybe I would keep my phone off all evening. Nothing life-changing had happened to me that day after all, but maybe the peace and quiet would be the life-changing thing? I could definitely handle more of it, take a break from dating, could I afford a few weeks off work?

I live in a bougie area. I have a pretty little one-bedroom in a six-floor pre-war building. It's a few blocks from the T. I passed a group of people chatting outside a bar, a woman texting. At the corner a cluster of well-intentioned boomers were drawing on pieces of posterboard. I couldn't see what they were writing, but honestly, I didn't try very hard. They were standing in front of a driveway blocked off with police tape.

That's when I heard my name shouted, not from the group but from the other side of the street. I didn't turn at first. My name is common enough it could have belonged to one of the neighbors. But then I heard it again, closer. Then something else: "Ich würde gern mit Ihnen sprechen." *I'd like to speak with you.*

I saw the man with no eyebrows first, Onions. It was such a shock that my immediate thought was *How did he get to my neighborhood so fast?* Though of course he'd had all afternoon to get here, just like I had. He had changed since the reading into a boxy gray suit. I had the immediate impression that what he had been wearing earlier was sort of a costume and that this was his *real* clothing. Next to him, a doppelganger. This guy had the same nothing-brown hair, he was maybe half an inch taller. Same suit. The most notable difference was the second one smelled like deodorant and he did have eyebrows.

"My associate and I want to know whether you've ever considered the foreign service?" **Eyebrows** said.

What the fuck?

"You don't know anything about me," I said. It was a reflex.

Eyebrows laughed.

"We know all about you. You think we'd approach you without vetting you? This is the first day you're meeting us, but this was not our first day observing you," Eyebrows said.

"Observing me?" I said. I tried to look affronted, but I felt flattered.

"Observing you," Eyebrows said.

I was dazzled. I thought about the mom spy, I thought about driving a McLaren. I thought about James Bond, except I was James Bond.

"How closely?" I asked.

"What?" Onions said.

"How closely have you been observing me?" I said.

What I really meant was "I know you don't know I'm a sex worker, and if you *did* know, you wouldn't be asking me this."

"Put it this way: We know who canceled on you this morning, and why he did it," Onions said.

So they *did* know I was a sex worker.

Even I didn't know why the client canceled on me. I was curious, but I decided not to ask.

Onions withdrew a card from his pocket and wrote on it.

Monday, nine a.m. On the other side: an address downtown.

"What is this?" I asked.

"An interview," Onions said.

I don't know what face I made. Based on their response, it must have been dubious or apathetic.

"We'll compensate you for your time, even if it's just the one interview."

I tried to nod in a way that conveyed a sense of "professional duh" while feeling completely surprised. Then, before I could say anything to mess it up, I shut my mouth and walked away.

My apartment was just as I'd left it, clean and warm. I liked to set up herbal tea in the morning to have at bedtime, and coffee at night for when I woke up. I put the kettle on and found the clump of neighbors out my window, still talking by the police tape.

I didn't know if I would show up for the interview. The prospect of a flashy new career was alluring, but if these guys were even the real deal, I had a feeling the only job I would qualify for was an entry-level cubicle position working for the people who got to do the cool stuff. Was that really worth it? Would I be willing to look at blurry truck images for long enough to dye my hair and orchestrate a high-level arrest? Or liaise? That was the other thing the woman had said women did in the foreign service. They liaised. What exactly did that mean?

I turned my phone back on. I had thirty-four texts, and a handful of missed calls from unknown numbers that I had a feeling all came from the same source: my morning client. I scrolled back to when I had turned off my phone.

I can use the deposit for when I reschedule.

Work for you?

?

Thinking maybe you could refund for now and I will pay the deposit again when I rebook. Work for you?

Thoughts?

Not trying to get out of it. Really was looking forward to this morning. Damn work!

Everything ok?

Hello?

Not sure if you're getting these.

Hey this is the time we were supposed to meet so I know you're not busy, could you just let me know this works for you?

Wow, ok, never mind. Just return my money please.

Guessing most of your clients don't need the money or this is nothing to them, but three hundred dollars is significant to me, I don't really have it to throw away, this is totally unprofessional.

Never had someone do this to me. Bad look.

Wow.

Nothing?

Ok.

I spoke to a friend of mine and without going into a lot of details I told him about the situation and he's shocked, he says you must not be very experienced, he said I can easily file a claim on the payment app to say the funds were stolen if you don't do the right thing, that would be a real pain.

I stopped reading and deleted the thread. I deleted the voicemails. I wired his money back to him. Almost immediately he texted again with smiley emoji, heart emoji. Thanks for understanding. Dot dot dot. Dot dot dot. A dick pic. I blocked him.

A cubicle might not be so bad.

From: Murder Bimbo
To: Justice Bimbo
October 18 at 7:11AM

Dear Justice,

That was the first part as quickly as I know how to tell it.

No one is here yet. The sun hasn't come up, but it's lighter out. Every once in a while I try to stretch my legs without making any noise. That's silly. I don't need to warm up. I doubt that the person coming for me is going to chase me. Most likely they'll either surround the place or shoot me on sight. I can't think about that, though.

I thought sending the first email would make me feel a little better. I thought this was going to be like carrying a whole lot of luggage. You start to feel better as soon as you put things down. Instead, it's like moving. You pack and carry boxes, furniture, knickknacks. And no matter how little stuff you think you own, no matter how much of the moving you've already done, it doesn't feel like you make any progress at all until you're completely done.

So I guess I have to take a sip of tepid water, stretch out my fingers, and keep going.

This is tricky because so much of this story includes sex work. And that's not a topic that the general public is very good at hearing about. Most of the time if you tell someone you're a happy sex worker, they think you're lying and if you tell them you're an unhappy sex worker, they think it's because sex work is a degrading profession you were forced into, so of course you're sad. You probably come from a broken home. That's a rough precedent to start with.

I'm hoping that because of your content, your listeners are sex-work literate, or at least not sex-work ignorant. Hopefully they know, like I'm sure you do, that there is nothing inherently sad about transactional sex.

People do it all the time. The sad parts of sex work don't come from the sexual nature of the work itself but from the systems around it: getting arrested for doing a job that is constantly in demand, doing that job without any benefits or safety net, and then feeling like even though you're working your ass off, you're the one who is supposed to be ashamed of it. Those things absolutely affect me. But most people think only abused and traumatized people become sex workers. The truth is, it's just a job like any other job.

I usually don't talk about my "past" to people outside the industry, because I feel like they are always listening for little clues about "how I ended up a sex worker." When they think they've found one, they cling to it and shape the whole story of my life around their interpretation. It makes it very hard for them to hear nuance or truth, because they are so sure that I have a Past instead of a past. Sometimes I do think it's gotten a little better, culturally. I used to date only sex workers or people who had already dated sex workers. But more civilians do understand it now. If you find the right ones, it's sometimes even nicer than talking to other sex workers, because they just listen and want to understand. Whether you've already been having this conversation with your listeners or you want to, doing an episode on me would really drive the point home. And that would be a net positive for all the sex workers out there, I think.

So I'll tell you about my past. It's only fair when I'm asking you to trust me, and I'm sure others will float alternate versions of my life story. People are going to want to blame me or make me out to be something I'm not. You have to know who you're dealing with.

It's up to you whether you want to share my background on the show. Obviously, I'm hoping this episode is going to reach beyond your normal listeners even, and you know better than me what will help "give me color" as opposed to what will lead listeners down the wrong path. I just finished saying how I don't like it when people question my job, and I get that this is your job.

I grew up in the Midwest. I tell people that my parents and I have different political beliefs because people buy it, but it's not actually true. My parents are pretty liberal. When I got my first girlfriend at sixteen, I thought they would be happy. My mom raised me in a very "you go, girl" home. For my eleventh birthday she bought me a little purple diary with "Boys Stink" in silver foil cursive on the front. I figured the more girls, the better. But she was cold to my girlfriend. It didn't make sense to me. My girlfriend was a long-haired tomboy with great grades who was super helpful around the house. Essentially, she was everything it had seemed my mother wanted *me* to be.

I asked her about it. I naively thought that maybe my mom just didn't like this particular girlfriend. I thought maybe she knew something about my girlfriend's family. Or maybe something had happened between them when I was in the bathroom. But my girlfriend said nothing happened. She said my mom seemed nice. *She may have seemed nice*, I didn't say, but I could tell she was being rude.

When I asked my mom about it, she literally shivered. Her face got very stiff. I hadn't considered for a second that my mom could be homophobic. But she was. She asked me if it was a phase. I could see she was hoping it was. I was very angry, and said no it wasn't, even though I wasn't sure myself. She asked me to be sure we didn't "do PDA" in front of her.

What happened next wasn't a single dramatic explosion.

My mom just sort of stopped being nice to me. It was like the stiffness she had about my girlfriend spread to me, too. When we were together, she stopped telling people she was my mother. I'm sure they could tell. We look alike. I only noticed this in retrospect. I promise you this sounds way more traumatic than it was. If we had disagreed over something and I felt guilty about it, maybe it would have hit me harder. I was so confident that being queer was okay and that she was wrong that I kind of felt bad for her.

One night we got into a fight unrelated to my girlfriend. It was just the kind of banal knock-down-drag-out nothing you have with your parents until you start having them with your partner. I wanted to leave. I told her I would spend the night at my girlfriend's house. She said fine. I left. The next morning, I went to school. By the time I got home, I had completely cooled off. But my mom had changed the locks on the doors.

I was sure she was just making a point. I knew the house was still my home; she wasn't kicking me out. She just wanted to continue our argument. But I didn't ring the bell. I didn't knock. I felt sure she could hear me trying to get in, but she didn't come to the door. I was a little hurt that she didn't chase me down. But everything hurts when you're a teenager, especially not getting chased by the people you love. I went over to my girlfriend's house. Her parents said I could stay as long as I wanted. At first it was a few nights. I ended up kind of moving in.

People are usually surprised this didn't do a lot of lasting damage to me or make me "incapable of love" or whatever. I think the thing was, I knew my mom was wrong. Some people would have the same experience and they would start to hate themself or think their queerness is bad. I never entertained those ideas. I just thought, *She's being a bigot, and I'm just me. I'm good.*

Through all of this, my dad stayed out of it. I understood that then and I still do. My mom needed someone on her side and that was literally his job. She and I sort of made up when I was about to leave for college. She didn't apologize, but she told me how much she loved me and that she didn't want to lose me as a friend. That's the only real scar the incident left—she still considers me a friend instead of a daughter. When I tell people my parents don't like that I'm queer, they ask if they're conservative and I let them think that they are.

I rarely visited home during college, not because I didn't love my parents but just because I was paying for everything on my own and there was never extra to make a trip. We began seeing each other more after I started doing sex work, because I had more cash. But we never really went back to how things had been. I never told them about my job because of the stigma. Now I think it's just normal that when you're a kid you're close to your parents, and then there's a rift of some kind. Mine was just a little earlier than other people's and about something kind of messed up.

I got into sex work when I was twenty-two. My brain had fully formed. It happened the way it does for a lot of people: I had been kind of adjacent to the field—that is to say, I worked in hospitality and I knew a bunch of sex workers, and I ran into an unexpected financial situation. I was a barista at the time, and my roommate was also a barista. We both worked a lot of hours and were part of the big, fun thing that happens in the service industry where all the workers know each other and hang out after closing and give each other deals. Life was really fun, but money was definitely tight.

One day we found an eviction notice on our apartment, even though we had been paying our rent in full every month. We called our landlord, but he didn't answer. In the morning we called the number on the eviction notice itself. The man on the phone had no idea who we were. He *said* he was the landlord, but he was definitely not the guy we'd been paying rent to for seven months.

"We've never been late, seventeen hundred dollars a month," I said.

He asked us what we thought our landlord's name was. We told him.

"That's the tenant!" he said. He told us the actual rent was $1,450. And that he hadn't been paid since a month after we moved in.

He told us he was going to have to evict the fake landlord.

"Can we just start paying you directly?" I asked.

"It doesn't work like that," he said.

"Can we have the place after you evict him?"

"Uh—I don't think so," the landlord said.

"What about our security deposit?" my roommate asked.

The landlord laughed. He hung up.

My roommate and I talked to legal aid, who told us that our best bet was to ask the landlord to rent us the apartment directly after he finished evicting the other guy. So we asked again, but he didn't want any part of it.

We had to find a new place. My roommate asked her parents for money, but I couldn't do that. We had a friend who was always talking about how she paid rent with feet pictures. I figured why not. I asked her how to do it.

When I realized that my face had to be in the feet pictures to actually make enough money, I felt both too embarrassed to back out and thrilled with the possibilities.

I made the money to move. Then I made enough money to go to the dentist and pay off some late doctor co-pays. Then I made enough money to start eating more produce. Then I made enough money to buy my friends pizza. The job expanded. Money had been lean for so long. I crept toward escort work slowly, always out of curiosity and desire. That was when I realized I was good at sex work and clients liked me. Within a year I had quit my barista job.

When people ask me how I got started, I usually say I fell into it, because it's true. Isn't that how you get into every job? An opportunity arises, you take it, it works out, you do it again, you get better. It's natural to grow in a role.

I have wondered if I'd ever tell my parents. I guess they're going to find out now. I seriously considered telling them shortly after this job started. I wondered if, twenty years into a career as a spy, I could tell them that before I went legit, I had been an escort. I would explain that it was actually the escort job that got me the spy job. Maybe that would declaw the truth. If it didn't, at least it would be overwritten by twenty years out of the trade.

When I read this back now, I admit that the story *does* sound a little depressing, but I swear it's not! I had a really happy childhood that wasn't ruined just because of a disagreement with my mother. That's not how life works: One thing going wrong doesn't ruin everything that came before it. Teenage years sucking doesn't negate the early years being good. And yes, I got into sex work because of financial need, but that's why people do any work! I'm not close to my family now, but a lot of people aren't, and maybe I will be again one day. We see each other a couple times a year because we live far away. If this was all it took to make someone a prostitute, we'd all be prostitutes! But since this is a sex worker's biography, it will get pulled apart and turned into trauma porn. Please remind your listeners not to do this. I know you get it.

From: Murder Bimbo
To: Justice Bimbo
October 18 at 8:50AM

Dear Justice,

This is taking too long. I reread the last email, and I think it's all necessary background, but I can't shake the feeling I'm running out of time. The wind has picked up. In the middle of writing the last email, I went outside to pee and almost had a heart attack when I heard a crunch in the brush. The crunch was the other end of the log I had leaned on, rolling into a pile of dry sticks. No one has come yet, so probably I wasn't followed, but they could still be tracking me. I wouldn't put it past them to tuck a tracker into something I ate. I am trying to remember whether I've chewed everything adequately in the last few days. There's been a lot of action and I'm prone to wolf things down. How long would it take for something like that to pass through my system? Or can it hang on somehow?! Enough.

I seriously hope you're getting these. When will you write me back? I clicked send on the last one before refreshing my inbox. I was so scared I would find a message from you telling me to cease and desist. I was scared my email would bounce back, blocked. It didn't, though. And nothing came. You probably haven't started reading, but I'm pretending that you have and that you're okay with me continuing, because I have to.

If I'm honest, I didn't expect I'd be doing sex work for as long as I have been. I've never had a desire to stop, but I've always felt like I should want "real work." Over time, I've applied to a lot of other jobs, especially in those first years. Most of the time I didn't get interviewed. I thought it was because I didn't have a degree, but then I started implying that I did have a degree, just to get to the first interview.

As my income and skill at sex work grew, so did my confidence that I could convince an employer to take a chance on me if they met me. But I still didn't get many interviews. I wondered if the problem was that I was aging but there were no new lines of work experience on my résumé.

Hopefully now you can understand why the idea of this interview was so invigorating. It felt like having a crush on someone when you're in a medium relationship. You thought things were fine, but now here's this new, hotter person who seems like a much better match for you than the person you're with. You're in your body again. You hadn't known you were out of it, but here you are again, and it feels so good.

Around me, I had watched baristas quit to become teachers, nannies go to social work school, bartenders law school. I noticed for the first time that all these service jobs were flush with kids in their early twenties, speckled with oddballs in their thirties and forties, and managed by lifelong smokers in their fifties. I had never thought about how that came to be until it started happening in front of me. The "real workers" got sifted out and the rest of us remained and aged.

Now I see the teachers and social workers stop at their old coffee shops on their way to school. They always get comped and always put the price of their order in the tip jar. They wear many scarves and smell of showers and vegetarian bacon sandwiches instead of beer and fresh coffee. Sometimes I want to become one of them. I definitely want health insurance and vacation days, and maybe even inane conversations with coworkers, and to find a sense of meaning in the work I'm doing. That sounds nice.

The morning after Onions and Eyebrows followed me home, I tried to go about my normal life but found myself inventing diagnostic questions. Was this what I wanted my life to be? If this existence ended, what would I miss? When I imagined my most fulfilled self, what did my life look like?

I was at the farmer's market when I realized just how many of my daydreams started with me falling into the kinds of careers people work years toward: teacher, nurse, writer, actor, wife. I thought I would just naturally become one of those people. But I didn't. I hadn't. No one tells you, when you're a kid, that choosing one thing means not choosing so many other things. Time is limited.

Maybe that reality fucked me up more than it fucked up other people, but I doubt it. I bet that's a common condition for a lot of the millennials who listen to your show. I bet a lot of them, if offered a new life, a structured life that seemed more like destiny than the random existence they'd cobbled together, would take it, especially if it felt epic. At least they would want to learn more. I wanted to learn more. Because while I had never planned to be an escort forever, I had also never imagined a proactive exit strategy.

I hadn't put this together until that very moment, and when I did, I almost puked on the carrots. Is that why I had accepted the card? Because I expected a deus ex machina to land me in the life I was destined to? And in every fantasy, without exception, I always had an attitude of graceful sacrifice. Sacrifice! Like sex work was a jewel that needed to be given up for a higher purpose only I could serve: the greater good, love, the kind of talent it was a crime to rob people of.

I had to go home soon if I wanted a nap before a date with my most regular regular at five. He was a nice enough guy. He was handsome, in his early forties, the kind of man who you would think is hot if he were a famous actor, but since he's a people manager at a biotech company he's normal. He was a fine guy, minus the way he always looked for opportunities to talk about his progressive politics in public. And he thought his politics made him a better client than a guy who tipped much better but who had conservative politics. I was "too smart to throw money at," he said he understood. Once he had gotten drunk and bragged to the rest of the patrons at the bar that I was a sex worker.

"I wasn't going to tell them you were MY sex worker," he said later. I gag to recall.

"There are other customers, snowflake," said a white-haired farmer with a box of radishes.

I plucked a bunch of radishes from the box and paid.

I'm going to try to get this job and see what happens, I decided, *and if that doesn't work, I'm going to come up with a plausible plan to leave escorting, not because I'm ready to go now but because I will be one day.*

Monday morning, I took the T downtown. The address on the card was an office suite in a high-rise with brown glass facades. I had done nothing to prepare besides googling what to wear to a government job interview (business attire, neutral colors) and plugging the address into my phone.

I drank a coffee in the plaza across the street from the building. I thought it would be a convincing touch if I could identify my interviewer on his way into work by a few subtle clues. How cool would it be to start the interview by telling my evaluator I knew who I'd be meeting because of the wear on his shoes or his tie clip or his coffee mug. I'd lay it out like a villain explaining his process in the final act. Unfortunately, Onions and Eyebrows didn't pass, and neither did anyone else who looked exactly like them or who looked like I guessed a spy might look. At 8:55 I entered the building, approached a U-shaped check-in desk where a woman in a navy suit scanned my ID, took my photo, and issued me a barcoded visitor pass she warned me would expire if I left the property. I rode the elevator to the ninth floor. Through a lit set of frosted glass doors, I could see the red stripes of an American flag.

I usually avoid interactions with any department/organization that might take my fingerprints or collect multiple forms of ID or put me into any kind of federal database. But this time I felt relieved when I saw the American flag. If the US government was going to hire me with full knowledge that I was a sex worker, didn't that kind of exonerate me from all my past crimes by making the government complicit, or declare me clemency or something? It would be the cleanest transition from one job to another, a transition where I would never have to worry about my old work coming back to haunt my new life.

That should say a lot about how naive I was.

Actually, the whole picture should. Based on an interaction with a man I had met at a lecture, who had never truly identified himself, I had convinced myself that I was being recruited to work as a secret agent. I would like to blame TV, but I blame myself.

At 8:58 a.m., I switched my phone to Do Not Disturb and went inside.

There were three other women milling behind the frosted door. Two were blond and bony and one was tall with black hair and violet contacts. I felt sure they were sex workers and was a little surprised I didn't know any of them from around. They may have been a couple years younger than me. Maybe they came up from Providence. The room itself looked like an office reception area, gray low-pile carpeting, a reception desk, and closed doors on two walls.

At 9:12 a man emerged from one of the doors with a stack of laptops. He opened them in a line on the reception desk, entered credentials, then handed one to each of us. "Minnesota Multiphasic Personality Inventory" the screen read.

One of the blondes rolled her eyes. The other opened her purse and pulled out a pen and notepad.

"You won't need that," the man said.

"Can we use our phones?" the first blonde asked.

The man shrugged.

"How long do we have?" the notebook blonde asked.

The man grimaced. It was a surprising face. He seemed genuinely shocked by the question. He looked up to the camera, then to the door, then to me. I shrugged.

"Half an hour?" he said.

I started right away.

I mostly told the truth, but when I didn't know the truth, I did try to pick answers that reflected well on me. For instance, I marked yes for "I have a good appetite" even though I often didn't, because I think people with a good appetite are more easygoing and probably make better coworkers. I also marked yes for "I have a great deal of stomach trouble," which wasn't true at all, but I didn't want to work anywhere where they wouldn't hire someone with stomach trouble.

When I was done, another man collected the laptops and brought up a new test. This time I couldn't see what it was called. After him, the first man returned. The entire morning was men, the glowing screens of laptops, the hum of fluorescent lighting, and the thunk of the climate control going off and on periodically.

I could tell what some of the tests were about: IQ, personality, geography. Another seemed like a blend of history and logic. There was a personal history questionnaire that asked generic life questions. There were questions about whether I'd been arrested or done anything illegal, but not about which specific illegal things I had done. I said yes, I'd done illegal things, because everyone should have said yes, I figured, even if the other women weren't sex workers or were lying about it, because at the very least everyone jaywalked.

For lunch they gave us thirty minutes in a courtyard with a turkey wrap, a Granny Smith, a four-pack of butter crackers, Sprite, and coffee. None of the women talked to each other. One of the blondes ignored her food and took a nap on a bench. I wondered if that was just a unique answer to whatever lunch was a test of. I wondered if she was the only one of us who was doing it right. If I hadn't gotten the impression the men were pencil-pushing bozos, I might have wondered if they were drugging us. I pulled the turkey off my sandwich and ate everything else.

After lunch they brought me into a small gray room with a drop ceiling, a desk, and four chairs. A man in a black suit with wraparound sunglasses showed me Rorschach blots and cartoon images. He gave me a pile of blocks to arrange and then a series of visual puzzles. He spoke more than anyone else, but still not very much. I asked him if he was a doctor and he laughed.

"PhD?" I said.

"We care less about traditional qualifications, more about efficiency," he said.

I nodded. He made a note, which seemed like a PhD thing to do.

When he was done with his tests, a tall man with white-blond hair and knuckles the size of walnuts came in.

Were the rest of the women still here? Had they made it this far? I imagined us each behind our own door, with our own **Walnuts**. How many of us did they need? What criteria were they using to select us? If this man was going to interview me, I thought, I had one chance to charm him.

"Nice to meet you," I said, standing up.

He smiled. He took my hand like it was funny that I'd offered it.

We sat.

"You're of German extraction?" he said.

"German and Scottish," I said. I thought he was making small talk. My last name sounded German. Maybe he was German?

"What about you?"

"I'm American," he said.

I went red.

"So am I," I said.

"I'm just teasing you," he said. Then he changed the topic.

"Thanks for your interest in our project," he said, "and for sitting through all of our formalities. I like to talk to all the candidates before they go, just to make sure they have a full picture of the job."

Wise, I thought.

"It looks like you scored off the charts in a few areas," he said.

"Oh?"

"Yes."

My palms itched.

"Good areas or bad areas?" I asked.

He chuckled.

He looked at his phone screen. I thought he was checking the time or his messages, but then he said: "Resourcefulness, personability, narcissism."

I smiled. Then I tried to politely convert that smile into a frown. He didn't seem to be paying attention.

"This job isn't for everyone," he said.

I tried not to nod too vigorously. I tried to arrange my face to look like the face of a person reconsidering the job with the plan to reject it, so that at the right moment I could change my mind and decide I was a perfect fit. But he was mostly looking at his walnut-knuckled hands.

"It can be dangerous," he said.

I imagined a car chase on the Amalfi coast. I imagined incapacitating an assassin at a casino in Monaco. I imagined protecting the president at all costs. Which, even though I wasn't a particularly patriotic person, seemed really cool and dramatic.

"I understand," I said stonily.

He didn't seem to hear that.

"It's a dangerous job. For women especially. As a woman there will be things you do on the job that a man wouldn't have to."

No shit, that's why you're interviewing sex workers, I didn't say. Someone knocked on the door, and before Walnuts could answer, Eyebrows was pushing in. He took the seat next to Walnuts. No one spoke.

"You did well," Eyebrows said.

Play it cool.

"Really? I wasn't sure. Good. I'm glad. Thanks," I said.

"We want to hire you," he said.

"Okay."

Eyebrows grinned. It was the first time I'd seen him smile and his teeth scared me. They were straight and bluish at the edges.

"You're just going to take any job?" he said.

I told him to fuck off. It was a reflex. A reflex I was proud of. He chuckled. He stopped himself. We were having fun.

"This is a polarized time in our country, do you agree?"

"Sure," I said.

"Democracy has rarely been threatened by so many different causes at once," he said.

I don't really know if that's true. I mean, I've heard people say it, and maybe? I just don't know enough about US history. It seems kind of hard to compare everything that's wrong with the country right now to everything that's been wrong with it at every other point in history. On the other hand, I could think of many things that seemed worse now than they'd been in a long time: white supremacy, for one.

"We are trying to fight those threats to democracy. Do you believe in America?" Walnuts said.

"Yes," I said. An enthusiastic yes seemed like the right answer. And because I knew I believed in doing what it took to get a secure job that you kinda liked that came with healthcare, and what was more American than lying to get one of those? And wanting to carry a gun. I had never considered carrying a gun, and I've always supported gun control, but I imagined having one legally and I could tell I would like the way it felt. That was American.

"Good," Eyebrows said. "You're a patriot."

That was the only thing anyone said that day that didn't feel right. It should have set off every alarm I had. Instead, I pretended we were just two people who liked different terms and one term he liked was "patriot," whereas I would say something more like "natural-born spy."

By the way, I *do* believe in democracy. Maybe that sounds dumb right after I told you about my relative political ignorance. I can't help it, though. Maybe it's because I grew up with it? Even though democracy has flaws, it just seems good and fair to me, and it seems like it should work, like the flaws are part of the system going wrong, not part of the system itself.

"There are two things you need to know about the job that might change your mind. First, this is not a desk job, and the project you'll be working on, there will be casualties. In fact, that's the goal."

"What do you mean?"

"Imagine you could go back in time and kill a homicidal maniac before they rise to prominence and kill a lot of people," he said. *Hitler*, I thought.

And that thought was correct, I mean, I didn't say it, and it wasn't actually confirmed for a long time. I mean, I didn't know *who* they meant to kill, but I understood it was a project to kill a rising political threat. I thought of three or four people it could be, but I wasn't sure who the government would see as enough of a threat to want to kill them. Meat Neck was on my list, but he didn't seem likely. Whoever it was, I hoped it had nothing to do with speaking Japanese, Italian, or German because I truly could not speak them.

"Okay," I said.

"Okay?"

"I think I know what you mean," I said.

"You are fine with that?" He looked surprised, offended even.

"I'm thinking about it," I said. "Anything else I need to know?"

"To be able to pull this off, you have to be willing to disappear."

I was about to ask what that meant. It chills me to remember that for an instant I did think he meant I would have to die. Maybe the fear showed on my face, because he clarified on his own.

"We will provide you with a new identity, after the job is complete," he said.

I didn't know exactly how I felt about that, so I tried to figure it out while giving no indication that I was trying to figure it out. Unfortunately that looked like me slowly nodding my head with very wide eyes looking off into the distance, which Eyebrows took as an affirmative. I went with it.

"And, pay?"

"Pay?"

"The salary," I said.

"Fifty-five k," he said.

There was another knock on the door and it swung open. Onions.

I smiled at him. I hoped he was going to join this tiny conference room clown car just for the story.

"We've got that call," he said to Walnuts.

"Sixty-five k," I said.

Walnuts frowned.

"Right, to be continued." He said this to me, but in the direction of Onions.

"I can take her out," Onions said.

Thanks for your time, I wanted to say. *I have some questions about the role I'd like to ask, what is your timeline for a decision, what are the next steps in the process*. But we were in the hall and Onions wasn't talking to me. At the American flag, he handed me an envelope.

"What's this?" I said.

"We won't meet here again," he said. "There's an address of our satellite office."

"An envelope for an address?"

"And remuneration for today," he said.

The envelope contained two hundred bucks. Not exactly what I was used to for a full day's work. I was disappointed and I'd like to say I wasn't surprised, but I was. They were lucky they had selected me. Would the other workers have even considered coming back for so little money? Only if they weren't doing it for the money.

I broke the first hundred on tofu bibimbap and did what I always did with cash: stowed 15 percent in a copy of *Candide* and counted out the rest for living expenses. That the pay sucked should have turned me off, but instead I kind of liked it. There was something so *real* about returning to a frugal life.

From: Murder Bimbo
To: Justice Bimbo
October 18 at 9:00AM

Dear Justice,

It makes me laugh to remember this now. I thought bare bones was romantic and now here I am. On the other hand, I thought that meager salary was bare bones, and acted like kind of a martyr about it.

Living on less didn't come back to me naturally, even though I'd lived that way a long time. And I don't exactly feel good, but the longer I sit here and the more I write to you, the stronger I feel. There was a reason these guys had found me. I have always been resourceful.

I peek out the window, scan the forest for movement. There is only a squirrel bounding over dry leaves. Through the window on the other side of the cabin I can see a mist sliding toward me.

One more chunk down, one more email closer to the whole story. I would like to take a nap. I would like to have something hot to drink. I'm wearing the only thing I could find on the way out of the city: yoga pants someone left in the hotel gym and a polyester button-up from a maintenance closet with a hotel logo on the breast. It can be so claustrophobic to wear other people's clothes.

What's next? I wish there were some quick way to give you an overview just in case. Since there's not, I'm worried I'm not being careful enough with the story. I've already told you more about my family than maybe I should have.

I googled you, by the way. I was halfway through writing the last email, and I just had to know a little more about the person I was pouring my life story out to. It turns out we have a lot in common. You're from the Midwest, too. Our birthdays are one day and one year apart (I'm older). We both took journalism in high schools named after presidents. We both hate gnocchi, are easily saddened by Robin Williams's death, and prefer the ocean to mountains.

I also found out you're married. That threw me. I guess when I started writing, I didn't really worry about implicating anyone else in the story. Either you'll tell her, and potentially make her part of my crime, or you'll keep it from her, creating a pretty big secret. I'm sorry to put you in that position.

It's even worse, because I googled her, too, and found out that she wrote that viral takedown of Meat Neck.

I remember that article. I read it when it came out. I remember he sued her for libel, and I know that even though it wasn't libel, she apologized, which made me think she was pressured. Maybe you won't want to touch this, because you're afraid of his cult of followers or don't want to stir up bad memories for her. Maybe you think opposing Meat Neck is a hopeless cause at this point. I hope not. I thought it was really cool of her to expose his assaults on sex workers over the years, after so much coverage about all the nonprofessionals he'd hurt. Sex workers owe her thanks. I know we feel it. I want this to be justice for her, too. I mean, it's awful, but it also means you're the exact person for this job. I wish I had known that going into this. But maybe that's just fate at work.

I hope the reason I haven't heard back from you yet is because it's early and you have a life. I wonder if you're staying in New York for a few extra days or if you're getting ready to leave for the airport. Maybe you caught the red-eye and crashed in your own bed just as I was arriving here.

I imagine your phone buzzing on the toilet lid while you take a shower. I imagine your email notifications on silent while you drive to the grocery store. I imagine you reading my email aloud to your wife and both of you thinking I am a scammer or a chump or a podcast-obsessed murderer.

"Maybe she uses humor as a coping mechanism," Wife says.

"Still, too dark," you say.

Maybe I haven't heard back from you because it's early, but maybe I haven't heard back from you because I've rung some kind of alarm in your body. In which case, I'm fucked.

I'm so worried I've framed this story wrong.

I just read everything I sent so far, and I want to clarify one thing.

I do hold myself responsible. I am only trying to tell you the story of what happened. I'm not trying to blame anyone but myself. Back in that Harvard/MIT lecture hall I had no reason to suspect that (1) anything weird was going on or that (2) at the end of the series of events I would kill Meat Neck.

I'm not saying I was tricked into doing what I did, or that if I had been omniscient then I wouldn't have done this. What I'm saying is that now, telling the story to someone else for the first time, I can see all kinds of little signs that things weren't quite right. In retrospect, it's kind of megalomaniacal to think that canceled client + spring day = I was destined for greatness. But like most humans, in the moment, I ignored the red flags. I saw things the way I wanted to see them. I made the choices I wanted to make.

The real question now is: If you do something great for the common good, don't the benefits to society outweigh the personal gain?

From: Murder Bimbo
To: Justice Bimbo
October 18 at 9:32AM

Dear Justice,

I officially started work a week after the interview.

The satellite office was a three-level duplex in Somerville with gray siding and an iron fence around a cement yard. The trees had completely leafed out. I thought it was pretty smart to set up shop in a dense and fairly diverse neighborhood.

"Everyone is through there," Walnuts said. He pointed up the stairs. The second floor was mostly kitchen with a screened-in porch, a dining area, and one small empty room where someone had posted a sign that read "Equipment."

Eyebrows, Onions, and Walnuts were all in the kitchen with a fourth man. Maybe he was forty. He was entirely bald and wore jeans and a faded black graphic tee. The graphic was a national monument montage: the Iwo Jima men raising a flag on top of the Vietnam veterans wall, next to the Jefferson Memorial rotunda, all under a crescent moon. **DC**.

"Welcome to the operation," Walnuts said.

Onions and Eyebrows sat at the table. I took an open seat across from them. DC stood.

"Surveillance," Walnuts said, pointing to himself.

"Comms." Onions waved.

"Logistics," DC said.

Eyebrows said nothing. Eyebrows was on his phone.

"Hey," said Walnuts, "workday has started."

"Heavy artillery," said Eyebrows.

DC chuckled. Onions smiled.

"Grow up," said Walnuts.

Eyebrows and Onions high-fived. I wanted to ask what his real job was, but everyone else seemed to know, so it felt like I should have already known, too.

For a government job, the team seemed more informal than I expected the CIA to be. Maybe they were NSA? How had I gotten this far without knowing who they were?

"What branch of the government are we with?" I asked.

"That's classified," Eyebrows said.

Was it legal to tell your employee that your identity as their boss was classified?

"How long have you all been working together before I joined?"

"That's classified," Eyebrows said.

Onions fiddled with a computer. He lowered the lights. A big blue square projected onto the wall. Everyone else seemed familiar with the blue square process.

"This is the Board. It's our source of truth. You have a question, come here first."

A professional portrait of Meat Neck popped up.

"Our assignment is the elimination of Meat Neck," Eyebrows said.

Meat Neck. Elimination. My mouth went dry. I had to stop my body from standing itself up. It wasn't that I wanted to leave. At least, I didn't think I wanted to leave. Actually, I did want to leave, but I also wanted to leap up and scream with joy. I was terrified—of helping to kill someone, of the danger inherent in that kind of thing, which I had actually NOT considered at the interview when they had urged me to. And of Meat Neck. Although if I had to be near him, the only way I would be able to stomach it is if I were there to kill him, so I was also elated. I was energized. Was I kind of bloodthirsty?

It was weird. If the target had been someone else, I wouldn't have been able to do it. I would have been out of there that day. I couldn't murder someone! But Meat Neck. Meat Neck had caused so much harm in the world already, and he wanted more.

The lady at the lecture had said nothing about deep ambivalence in covert work. But she had talked about feeling unprepared and pushing through, and I definitely felt unprepared.

I was very nervous. Maybe I *had* been too hasty accepting the job. Fortunately, nervousness and regret are a common enough combo in my line of work. I swallowed them both and tried to respond with bravado until the feelings were over.

Walnuts made an explosion gesture with both hands.

"When?" I asked.

"Before November," Eyebrows said. "Any more questions?"

I knew he meant "Shut the fuck up."

"Why?" I said.

"Excuse me?" Eyebrows said.

"Why are we doing it?" I said.

"That's classified," said Walnuts.

The men looked bored. All of this was rote to them.

"It's okay," said Onions. Maybe he felt protective because he'd brought me in. More likely he wanted to keep me in line so he wouldn't look like he backed the wrong candidate.

"He's a threat to democracy," Eyebrows said.

The others nodded. *Fair enough,* I thought. Meat Neck was a threat to democracy. I just hadn't expected a government agency to agree with that, or at least not to come right out and say it.

There was so much I didn't know. I decided to try something I hadn't tried yet. I shut up, paid attention, and gave the guys the benefit of the doubt.

Once we got to work, the informality of those first minutes evaporated. Eyebrows oriented us back to the Board. The Board was a sort of digital fact tree assembled, edited, and maintained by him. It contained all the components of the job we needed to consider: schedules, relevant news pieces, locations, options. Outstanding questions were in red. Eyebrows could animate portions.

They called my role "front of house." I guess they felt squeamish calling me bait to my face. But I wasn't squeamish about it. Someone would have to get Meat Neck off on his own and I was sure I could handle it. I don't know if this is a thing for other jobs, but in sex work, I'm really used to being on the thin edge of something. One side is danger and one side is triumph. So it's weird to say, but it was the fear that made me feel comfortable. It was a familiar fear that I knew how to work through. It was a little more extreme, because Meat Neck wasn't just some regular john. And it was more intense, because the act on the table was murder instead of sex. But I could fake it until I made it.

More troubling was the whole "disappearing" that I was supposed to do. That particular piece had been blinking in the back of my head ever since they said it at the interview. I had said I was willing to do it, but no one had stopped to explain how. Had I implied I already knew how? I didn't want to ask.

I waited until Eyebrows raised the topic again, which came a few weeks in. It turned out I didn't exactly have to "disappear." In fact, the less like a disappearance my disappearance was, the better, they said. I needed to look like I moved away, severed ties, ran off to start a new life somewhere. If I had been gone for months before the assassination, then it couldn't have been me who had done it. I wasn't around. If I just dropped out of my life the morning of the act, that would be a huge red flag.

It was DC's job to work on the disappearance plan with me. We needed something that was realistic, that people who knew me would believe.

"Maybe I'm leaving because of a bad relationship," I said.

"We don't need the why, we just need the how."

I had seen enough true crime to feel we needed a why. If we didn't have a why, someone might keep looking for me.

"No one is going to keep looking for you," DC said. His face was steady. What did he mean?

I got the sense that DC already hated me. Either for no reason or a gut reason or, I worried, because I was a sex worker. That's who no one goes looking for, right, sex workers?

"We are going to make sure they have other things to worry about, is what he means," said Walnuts.

I still thought he was underestimating true crime girls, but I was practicing shutting up.

"I think Mexico," DC said.

I had never been, but I liked the idea.

"How is your Spanish?" Walnuts asked.

"Un poquito," I said.

DC grimaced.

"Canada?" said DC.

"How's your hiking?" Walnuts asked.

"Great," I said.

My hiking *was* great. I love the outdoors. Before I'd left college, I'd even taken a PE credit in orienteering. DC had an atlas. We got to work. The plan was that I would pack up my apartment and stage a move to Canada. I would drive up in August, cross the border with my real passport, leave the car somewhere TBD, and walk back across the US border.

"It's the longest unguarded border in the world," Walnuts claimed.

I didn't fact-check that. When you're collaborating with men, I always find it's easier to only fact-check things that are pertinent to the work. If you start questioning whether they're right about irrelevant things, pretty soon you're lost in a thought experiment run by a devil's advocate for the edification of no one. We didn't need the longest unguarded border, we just needed enough room to get across.

It took a few weeks to build the full plan. It would have gone faster if DC had listened to me more often, but I was just the new girl on the job, emphasis on "new," emphasis on "girl," so why would he? I learned pretty quickly it saved time to just let him drive. DC would have an idea and we would talk through how to do it, see if it was possible. Then we would list out everything that could go wrong and come up with solutions. What if someone recognized me? What if there was a snowstorm? What if I got lost? What if I ran into someone I'd never met, but who didn't like the look of me? What if I got lost later, at a different part of the plan? Or hungry or tired? Every so often I tried to toss in a more exciting scenario: What if I met a pack of wolves? What if there was already a different team there, and I noticed them one night at the opera, and they were sent to intercept us because we had a mole? What if I was on my hike and I ran into a hypnotist? What if something happened on a high-speed train? At first he answered them earnestly, but he caught on fast.

Basically, DC thought I was a child. Sometimes it was me who had an idea, but he would "brainstorm" until he hit upon whatever I had already said, often in strikingly similar language. Did he not hear me when I suggested it? I wondered if *he* was trolling *me*. I wanted to make a friend to talk to among my new coworkers about this, but the guys were busy with work all day. Sometimes we broke for lunch at the same time, but then everyone was there. DC, too. So I was left trolling DC alone, for my own benefit. One day when he was answering my joke as if it were a serious question, it occurred to me that he might be neurodivergent? I felt bad. I was going to apologize, but then he took a call from his boss, so I didn't have a chance.

While I worked with DC, the other men worked together. They started at nine and no one left before five thirty. They were professional, tidy, diligent, and only humorous during breaks.

The Board filled with information: names, addresses, photos, family trees, biographies, aliases, research, citations, and new questions. Soon it was a collage of black columns that each terminated in red unknowns. Whenever anyone got discouraged, Eyebrows would remind them to focus not on deleting the red but on extending the black, on breaking questions into smaller questions versus solving the whole puzzle.

Though I mostly worked on my disappearance, I tried to make suggestions about other stuff on breaks. I absorbed as much as I could. Somewhere in my very noncorporate brain there was a phrase rattling around about doing your boss's job before you're promoted, if you want the promotion.

They worked out murder method possibilities, then cross-planned with locations. They looked very hard, I think, to find a way to reach Meat Neck in his home. When that proved impossible, they settled on a party at a hotel.

Just because I believed Meat Neck was bad for the country doesn't mean I didn't have critiques of the team. I thought they were generally misogynistic in that way where you couldn't point it out without seeming too sensitive. I thought their politics weren't very nuanced, or maybe they were too nuanced, in that the views they expressed seemed contradictory. But I loved the plan. It was just as romantic as I'd hoped. DC would pick me up once I crossed into the US and we'd drive back to Somerville, where I'd take the upstairs bedroom at the satellite office until the job was over.

It only took a few weeks of 65k before I had to road test the fantasy of returning to a frugal life, a spartan aesthetic. Honestly it was hard. I could have picked up a client or two, but it would have completely gone against the initiative to disappear. Plus, in my short time off, I'd grown more sensitive to the bullshit you have to deal with in even the easy interactions of sex work. I didn't think I'd have the emotional resources to act stable/hot with a client, then be my best self at work. The guy I'd have been most likely to call was the progressive regular I'd seen right before the whole thing started. And these days he was showing real signs of a breakdown. When I'd told him I was taking time off, he'd found a way into my buzzered building and started leaving "gifts" on my doormat: frozen Omaha steaks he could text me about "so they didn't melt," Klonopin he got from a "source" (pretty sure it was his own prescription), a black striped swimsuit designed for surfers and two sizes too small. In a way, I was doing this for him, too, because seeing Meat Neck rise in the polls seemed to actually be making him lose his mind.

In the beginning of June, DC and I sat down to make a list of everyone I knew. This was the final step of my disappearance. The house had been loud all week with guys moving boxes into the equipment room. I never tried the door. I didn't care about equipment. I felt sure that I was being tested, though, and kept track of every temptation I resisted.

"We have to think of everything, all the people you know, all the people you don't know, but who know you."

"What does that mean?" I asked. A clatter in Equipment. Cursing. Onions shouting that he was okay.

"People who would recognize you," he said.

"Oh, like baristas," I said.

"Exactly."

"Well, that's easy. I'll just change my hair and makeup, and if anyone acts like they recognize me I'll tell them they're wrong," I said.

DC did not believe this would work.

"Even if I don't change anything at all, it would work," I said.

"How would that work?" he said.

"People are embarrassed to be wrong and even more embarrassed to be forgotten," I said.

"I'll think about it," he said.

Meanwhile I made my pathetic list: my parents, a neighbor, a bartender, a few others.

"On October seventeenth, we don't want any of these people surprised that they can no longer reach you. It can't feel sudden, or if it feels sudden, it has to feel sudden long before October seventeenth."

"I get it," I said.

"Are you sure this is everyone?" he asked.

I looked back at the list. Unless October 17 was the size of 9/11, none of them would think to check on me.

"I could include exes," I said.

He literally scoffed. And in that moment I knew he didn't know any queer people.

From: Murder Bimbo
To: Justice Bimbo
October 18 at 10:45AM

Dear Justice,

I've only been in love-love once. We were no longer in touch by the time DC told me I needed to cut contact with everyone. But if I had listed the people who reliably worried about me, she would have been at the top of the list.

I was twenty when we met. She was thirty. It was that shining kind of desire that makes you realize all other attraction has made you feel less like yourself, while real love has the power to make you feel the opposite.

We met online, and both expected it to be nothing, a one-night stand. It was so not-nothing that we forgot to even talk about it.

After our first date I went home in a strange, liminal frame of mind. It could have been the hangover or staying up all night, but whatever it was, the city hummed and my body felt immune to pain.

I thought, *This is the last morning I'll be single.*

I bought a coffee and a bag of pistachios and walked a loop around the commons, basking in the kind of solitude you can get only when you are deeply loved.

When I got home, I reread messages from a few people I'd been flirting with online and the excitement had burned off them. Was it better to say I'd met someone? Stop responding?

I'd used other excuses in the past, told people I'd be leaving town or I'd reconnected with an ex, would be in touch later.

This time I just deleted my accounts.

For the next two years, I did everything I could to impress her. My desire to do this never diminished. When I succeeded, I only grew more desperate. I wanted her to adore me in every way. I learned to play the guitar, rock climb, cook Thai food. I learned to like the bands she liked, and I read every book she ever mentioned. I didn't feel like I lost myself in this process; if anything, it just made me more sure of who I was, having her as my foil. I knew I would never get tired of her. I knew our love would continue to grow. I knew, if we stayed together, we would both continue to love each other even as we changed and our relationship morphed. I knew we could have been together forever.

We fought sometimes but they were the kind of big fights you have only with your closest friends or yourself. No matter how intense they were, they never threatened our connection or made either of us doubt we were made for each other. "Made for each other." We thought like that. We talked like that.

Then it ended. For years I developed elaborate theories about why, dramas I thought matched the strength of our connection. But I'm older now. The truth is, it just ended. We were at different places in our lives. Ten years was a bigger chasm than either of us understood in the beginning.

After we broke up, she was single for a year, "heartbroken and waiting," she said. I dated other people. Many. Then one day she called to let me know she had met someone else. There was nothing I could say. I hoped it wasn't serious. But she wouldn't have called unless it were. I asked if this person was a better match for her than me and she said yes. I had asked it as a blade to stab myself with, so I wouldn't want her so badly. But it didn't work like that. I wanted her more.

Our lost love festered in a way it hadn't after we'd originally broken up. It became an ache any strong emotion could reactivate. Too happy? Pain. Too sad? It reminded me of her. Anger? Felt like our fights. I practiced ignoring it. I learned to have quieter feelings in general, none when possible.

She married.

There was something about her face in the wedding photos I had never seen before. Sometimes during the worst moments, I told myself it was a seed of apathy, proof she was faking it with the new woman, but I knew it was a peace she had never had with me.

After a couple of years, my feelings changed again, and I began to feel happy for her. For them both. At first it was only when I reminded myself of all the facts of their love. But with practice it got easier, and after the first instance of happiness it took only a couple months before I was delighted for them. Thinking about them as a couple relieved me.

I never think of her in any way except as someone else's now, and it always cheers me up.

I don't know if this is messed up, but I feel pride about their love, almost ownership for it. They couldn't have happened if we hadn't failed first.

I am telling you all of this because I want you to know that I am capable of great love and connection. I am not disposable. No one is, but I'm not, either. Please don't let people forget me.

When all this assassination stuff started I just so happened to be in a place in my life where none of my loves were actively reciprocal. I was less connected to people than I have been at other times.

I'm so scared that because of that, when they find me, they'll kill me and no one will notice. And I am also telling you this to let you know that despite what comes next, I am just a human at the center of this story, doing her best, with messy feelings. I did what I did next because I'm a person.

From: Murder Bimbo
To: Justice Bimbo
October 18 at 11:20AM

Dear Justice,

When I wasn't at the house in Somerville, I cleaned out my apartment. I sorted my things into save and toss. I carried bags to the dumpster, to the big clothing donation vessel at the end of the block that was probably a scam. I left my food processor on the corner.

My diet changed, too. At first it was more takeout, which felt good to eat because at the end of the meal you can clear all the evidence into the trash. It made it feel like I was always making progress toward downsizing my household. But takeout quickly became too expensive. The salary I was given was enough to cover rent and utilities, but not much more. I cooked rice and beans, bought day-old bread, gave up the farmer's market. My body felt worse, but I identified that, too, with a cleansing transformation.

All this food talk. You don't need to know what I was eating! I'm just hungry. I skipped dinner last night because I was too anxious, so all I've had since yesterday's lunch is a protein bar and a sleeve of gas station Donettes.

It was my ex, actually, who had first introduced me to Meat Neck. Not literally, of course, but as a character. I had heard of him, but I hadn't paid any attention to him. I thought he was a vocal former athlete I didn't like the look of.

"He's dangerous," she said.

We were showing each other video clips in bed, of things we liked and things we had opinions on. It was still the beginning of our love.

"He's no one—a lot of athletes are Republican," I said.

She maintained he was different. He did two tours in Afghanistan and for a long time he didn't talk about it, but then he started talking about it constantly.

"He's going to jump to politics," she said, like he was a forest fire approaching a highway.

"He's so young, no one will take him seriously," I said. But his youth was like every other factor I raised. She swore it made him more dangerous, not less. He had so much time ahead of him, he was handsome, no one could accuse him of being outdated. He claimed his was a new kind of conservatism. It may have been. I'm not an expert.

When a congressman in a state where he had a home (not even his main home) died, and he ran to fill it, I didn't think he would win. My ex did, though. When he won, I still didn't care.

"He's going to see how hard politics is and he won't run again," I said.

"He is going to get high on all his constituents," she said.

"They're crazy, they're no one, it's not like the NFL," I said.

"It doesn't matter. Attention is attention, and sometimes it even feels better if it's from someone who is completely out of their mind."

I couldn't deny that part.

But I didn't think the people would stand for it. I really didn't think Americans would support a fascist, which is what my ex called him.

"His fans will *love it* if he is excessive. It will mean they don't have to be evil, because he's got it covered. It will mean they can be if they want to be, because he's the new norm."

"Which is it?" I asked, pleased to catch her failure in logic.

She shrugged. She didn't look chastised. She looked disappointed in me.

Then, six months later, it turned out I had been right about him not running again. He said that politics wasn't for him. He disappeared from public life, or the public life I paid attention to. My girlfriend grew morose.

"I thought this was what you wanted," I said.

She shook her head. She stopped talking about him with me. She stopped talking about Meat Neck almost at all, except on the rare occasion that another anti–Meat Neck zealot offered a perspective before she had a chance to. When that happened, she would disappear into a corner with them, getting drunker, angrier. She was convinced that he wasn't retired, but hibernating, and that his return would be huge. She became an encyclopedia of his crimes. It was the only thing that gave her any solace. I tried to simultaneously ignore and support her obsession. This was something that, at the time, I thought was unique and clever of me. Now I'm older and I realize it's just a very basic part of all relationships.

Anyway.

We had been broken up for years by the time Meat Neck announced he was running a third-party presidential campaign. She texted, **Have you seen this?** A poster with his face on it: tight-shot, angry.

I hope one of his hookers kills him, I replied.

I had recently quit my barista job and started relying on full-service sex work as my only source of income. It had lit all kinds of fires under me, and I was striking out with force in all directions. I was angry and brave in new ways, in ways that didn't always make sense when I looked back on them. Sometimes I was right, though, by coincidence or gut feeling, I still haven't bothered to figure out.

My text started a fight between us about the word "hookers," which honestly might have been why I sent it, to use the word, to start the fight, to push her away a little, to show her she was already further away from me than she thought she was.

I was proud to be a sex worker, and I also blamed her for it because the alternative could have been that we were a happy couple somewhere and—I didn't know what the "and" was, but it seemed like the things I hated about my life definitely weren't my fault.

Meat Neck lost.

He didn't even draw significant voters away from either candidate. But something did happen. "Communities" developed on the internet, cesspools really; people who had been politically agnostic all their lives switched on. Only a very tiny fraction switched on *against* Meat Neck. By the next midterm election, the country had changed. Mainstream news picked it up: the first major spike in voter turnout since, well, they couldn't agree on since when, but it was big.

The more insane shit he says, the more people like him, she texted.

We were not supposed to be talking. It was midnight. She was probably drinking. She had told me she wasn't going to text me anymore. Her wife didn't like it, and she didn't like it about herself. She didn't like the version of herself she was with me. She said this in a way that made me feel like it was my fault.

I poured my own drink. I tried to think. I stared out the window. I cried, but decided it was out of rage instead of loneliness.

I know I gave you shit before. Deep down, I thought I was wrong and you were right. I really thought if he got crazy enough, he would lose people. But it's not working like that, she said.

I had never heard her give the American people the benefit of the doubt like that. I thought she distrusted them. But maybe I was actually the one who distrusted them. Maybe it was the effect of a few years of sex work. People told me stuff they wouldn't normally say out loud and I'd learned that most men were worse than I'd have guessed.

I didn't respond to the texts this time, by the way. I wanted to, because I didn't agree with them, and I wanted to because I wanted to talk to her. But I respected her relationship with her wife, and her wife didn't deserve to feel like shit just because we both got drunk and started ranting about Meat Neck. Instead I opened the texts, over and over, drafted responses in my head. When it felt too hard to resist them, I took screenshots and deleted the conversation, as if that would fix it.

From: Murder Bimbo
To: Justice Bimbo
October 18 at 11:55AM

Dear Justice,

On a hot August morning I loaded a red Camry purchased by DC with three large cardboard boxes of clothing, a crate of books, and a small duffel bag containing all the clothes I would need for the trip, as well as a hiking pack, water bottle, and $500. I left the car double-parked in front of Dunkin' long enough for people to come in to complain. I complained about the complainers to the staff. I tried to look a little wistful so that they would remember seeing me.

"I'll miss this," I said to the teenager who handed me my medium hot regular.

She looked confused.

The wistfulness had been DC's idea. I had thought it was dumb. I had to stop listening to him. He wasn't the one who'd scored remarkably high on the personability test.

At nine a.m., I got in the car and left.

Nothing happened on the drive. I listened to an audiobook. I spent an embarrassing amount of time imagining scenarios where I had to hack into the MI5 headquarters. I stopped for the night on the American side of the border. I could have made it in one day, but everyone agreed it would be better if I stopped and let some strangers know I was leaving the country.

"Make someone earn your confidence, then admit that you're leaving the US," Onions had said.

I didn't think Onions had earned anyone's confidence in his life, after his mother's.

I went to sleep in a three-star motel that the desk clerk assured me had a functional waffle maker in the lobby.

I should mention this all happened on the evening of August 4. You know what happened the next day. I was on the road when I heard.

Breaking news out of Pittsburgh: Three gunmen apprehended and another escaped after shots were fired at Meat Neck outside his preferred fast casual restaurant. Meat Neck sustained no injuries, but had reportedly not ducked. Sources reported a favorability bump. Then Meat Neck made a statement that he was not afraid, that he was protected by God (who he still claimed he barely believed in, but knew his followers did), that he was declining additional protection.

By the afternoon his additional popularity was a story of its own. Previously undeclared businessmen, country musicians, and comedians were declaring that they loved Meat Neck. "Meat Neck is a hero!" they said. "Meat Neck is a real American!" Radio programs unearthed nonvoters to announce their conversions. They aired third-rate talking heads speculating on whether Meat Neck could substantively reinvigorate the youth's passion for voting.

I worried. What did this mean for me? For the whole operation? Would our plan still be possible? Was it canceled?

And more questions: Did the Somerville guys know the people who orchestrated the assassination attempt? Was it another country? Or criminals? Would that group try again, and maybe be successful before we could get to him? What if the new association of violence against Meat Neck by criminals deterred the government, and we got shut down? Even if he was saying no to increased security, surely it would be harder for a random person to get close to him after this. Why hadn't it occurred to me that other people would be out there with the same idea? I was embarrassed.

In most of the scenarios I thought up, I got fired. I would return to Massachusetts and have to go back to my old life. Because I was disappearing, I didn't have a phone on me and I had no idea what to do. I could keep going, but there was a chance no one would be waiting on the other end to pick me up.

The closer I got to the border, the faster the thoughts came. No single idea took precedence. I guess I just never had one strong enough to turn the car around, so soon enough I was crossing the border, saying to myself: *If I find myself alone in a forest on the border, I can get home—I can get anywhere. Even if the job is over and the guys ditch me, I am a changed person now.* The job had changed me. I had changed myself. I would build another life if I needed.

The border crossing was uneventful. The next leg of the drive was as well. I won't tell you about the details. It took me between one and twenty-four hours to get to the place where I would cross the border. I'm not trying to provide a map for anyone else. And it doesn't really matter. What I will say is that it was evening when I left the car in a barn DC told me would be there, walked a mile along a farmer's tree line, then moved into the woods. I wasn't scared. Maybe I should have stayed there. Almost certainly I should have stayed there. In Canada, I mean, not the woods.

Once I'd crossed back into the US, I had to hike several miles to a highway. It was actually a really nice hike. I remember thinking, if DC comes to get me, that's great. I am ready to get back to work. If he doesn't get me, maybe this is the start of a different kind of life. It's funny to be here now, in a similar landscape but with a completely different uncertainty. I wish I were still there. I wish DC hadn't come after all. But he did. And because I still didn't know what was coming, I was happy to see him.

DC was happy, too. In fact, he was giddy. It turned out the team had an optimistic read on the attempted assassination situation.

"He's declared open season on himself," DC said.

He swiped his phone and handed it to me. The news.

"'Meat Neck says come and get me,'" I read aloud.

"'Record number of groups take credit for knowing about assassination attempt.'

"'Meat Neck team confirms they will not increase security.'"

We drove straight back to Massachusetts. I tried to sleep, but all I could manage was a drowsy gaze out the window. When we pulled up to the house in Somerville, DC parked and got out with me.

From: Murder Bimbo
To: Justice Bimbo
October 18 at 12:24PM

Dear Justice,

I was officially a fully-fledged anonymous government agent living in a partially finished attic, up a flimsy spiral staircase behind the kitchen of the house that served as our mission's home base. I had a narrow bathroom with a tight shower, and only left my space during work hours.

A few days after I returned from Canada, we met for our weekly team meeting.

"Doughnut day," Eyebrows announced when I came down. It was Friday.

This was the only day of the week when the men were all routinely in chatty moods. We ate doughnuts until Walnuts finished his announcements and updates. I remember I was tired that morning, maybe a little grumpy. I took a maple glazed to a chair.

"We have a credible opportunity," Walnuts said.

We all stopped chewing. This was what we had been working toward, but the breakthrough felt like it came out of nowhere.

Walnuts flicked through photos on a tablet and held up one of Meat Neck in a tuxedo at a party. My maple glazed turned to sawdust in my mouth.

"We'll have a two-hour window in New York," he said.

DC nodded. Everyone nodded.

"A crypto event."

I tried to swallow but the sawdust had turned into cement.

Eyebrows put the Board on the wall. It was crammed with text too small to read without zooming in. Very little red remained.

"Onions is going in as a cater bartender," Walnuts said. "Eyebrows is working security."

That made sense. Eyebrows was the beefiest guy we had.

"DC will be a gala guest," he said.

"What about you?" I asked.

"Techie," he said.

"Yeah, he's the nerd," Onions said.

"I prefer 'hacker,'" Walnuts said.

"When Onions starts his shift, he is going to notice that they don't have enough Grey Goose for the evening. He's going to get a case from the liquor store around the corner and smuggle a pharmaceutical vial back in with him."

"Why can't he just bring it with him to work?" I said.

"Security is too high: They pat down all the employees working these events," Onions said.

"Okay, but then won't they check when you come back?" I said.

"We're going to put the drugs in the vodka box and glue the case shut so it looks like it came straight from the factory," he said.

I didn't think that would work, but Walnuts was beginning to look irritated by my interruptions, so I stopped.

"So the bartender," I said.

"Me," Onions interrupted.

"Yes. You are going to serve him a poison drink? In the middle of a fundraiser?" I said.

They all laughed, Onions the most.

"Not quite. We have to get Meat Neck into a private room. We're not trying to get arrested," they said.

"Arrested? How would you be arrested? Wouldn't you just tell the cops, I don't know, that we're the government?" I asked.

"I wish it worked like that," Walnuts said. "The government doesn't just have carte blanche to kill someone. You can thank Ronald Regan for that," he said.

"Ronald Regan made murder illegal?" I said.

"Executive Order 12333 says 'no person employed by or acting on behalf of the United States government shall engage in, or conspire to engage in, assassination.'"

"Oh," I said, "well, okay, so if I or any of our team is caught or killed, the government will disavow any knowledge of our actions?"

DC chuckled.

No one else responded.

"Don't mind me, just asking questions," I said.

"Are you done?" Eyebrows said. I shrugged. I was so annoyed by being ignored that I didn't fully process what they had just told me.

"You will pass by Meat Neck in the lobby. He will see you go, wait, and follow you out. I will make sure the cameras between the gala and the suite are off. The hotel won't have any cameras in Meat Neck's room, but he might, so we need to be careful."

"He's just going to see me and feel he needs to follow me?"

"Of course not. He's prepped. He's been texting with you and you have a date," Eyebrows said.

I desperately did not want to see the texts that Eyebrows was sending in my name. It was well-known that Meat Neck had a taste for a certain kind of escort.

"Older," the paper called them, "plain Janes."

"But you won't go directly to his room," DC said.

"No?"

Eyebrows enlarged a section of the Board. I wanted to help kill Meat Neck. But the plot was beginning to sound insane, overly complicated, and far-fetched. It would make more sense for me to just try to pick him up at the bar—get him up to his room or even into a bathroom for a quick hit of coke and one of the men could come in to finish the job. Maybe that would have been too messy for the government?

DC would accompany me in as my "handler." We would stop on the way at Walnuts' room to pick up the poison. I waited for them to turn to me so I could tell them that was a dumb idea. Like truly nuts. I would not bring a "handler" to a date. Maybe I would bring the kind of driver who was also muscle to the hotel lobby? But probably not. Worse, they wanted DC to stay in the suite with us. *If I am playing myself on this mission, just ask me*, I thought.

They argued for a while over whether Meat Neck would let DC stay in the suite. Some said no because he would want privacy, some said yes because he wouldn't care. *It will depend on what he's into*, I didn't say. That is, if he hasn't seen through this "handler" plan already. If anyone brought me in, it should be another worker, someone he already knows. That's who men trust to recommend other escorts.

Either way, I would be fine, they all agreed. Even if DC left, I would be alone with Meat Neck for only ten minutes. Eventually they agreed, without my intervention, that DC could bring me to the hotel suite door but would not actually go in. It wasn't because it was unrealistic, though. It was because Onions and Walnuts thought if DC got that close to Meat Neck, he'd be tempted to finish the job himself.

I would offer to make drinks. Did I know how to make a martini, they wondered but didn't ask me. I would make him a martini using the vodka in the room. I would need to add 300mg of Metildigoxin that I would withdraw from a pharmaceutical vial using a syringe. Did I need a tutorial on using a syringe, Walnuts asked DC.

So my only task was putting poison in a martini and handing it to Meat Neck? Why was I even necessary? Why couldn't a waiter bring a dosed martini? Why did they need bait at all? Maybe they thought Meat Neck wouldn't accept a drink from a man? More likely, I figured, I was just learning what it felt like to be part of a bureaucracy. Four men and one woman working full-time to do something a non–government worker could do in an hour. But I didn't want to be fired.

"You don't have to let him touch you," Walnuts promised.

They were all looking at me then.

"What happens after?" I asked.

The men looked relieved. I realized they had been worried about telling me the specifics of the assassination plan. Maybe they thought literally planning the murder would freak me out? I don't know. I wondered what would have happened if it had. What does the government do in situations like that? Would they lock me up until the operation was over? Or would they trust me to keep the mission quiet? They could kill me, I realized. Technically, I had already disappeared. But I didn't actually think that was a serious possibility. Not that day.

"That's easy: You stay with him until you're sure he's dead. When you're absolutely sure, call the front desk. The front desk will call an ambulance.

They are going to tell you to stay where you are. You leave, and meet DC at a predetermined location—" Walnuts said.

"The mezzanine," said DC.

"We're still working on the details, but probably the mezzanine," Walnuts said.

"What if I'm caught leaving?" I asked.

"You'll say you were there for a date, you had drinks, and he said he needed a nap. When he didn't come out of the bedroom, you went to check and he was dead."

"Do I tell them I'm an escort?"

"No, try not to. They will probably guess, but that's fine. They'll figure it out and assume you were lying because of that."

"They won't know it was poison?"

"It will look like a heart attack, and his people will want to sweep the details under the rug. They won't mention a hooker unnecessarily."

"And what about after?" I said.

"Once we're done, as soon as we're done, everyone else leaves. Bartender gets an emergency phone call from his girlfriend, security walks off the property. I'll come back in to meet you," DC said.

The men were all around me then, waiting for my reaction.

"Other questions?" Walnuts asked.

I had plenty of questions they couldn't have answered, like what I should wear to a fundraiser. And I had questions they wouldn't want to hear, like, can I offer you some constructive feedback on the "handler"? And I wanted to know what would happen after it was all over, how long I needed to disappear and whether there would be another operation after this one, but they seemed a little doubtful about my competence and I didn't want to feed that. And I wanted to know why the plan was so overly complicated in places and simple in others, and why it had to be poison and why they needed a sex worker at all. But I knew the answer to all those questions, and the answer was that these guys were government employees who had learned everything they knew about sex workers from *Law & Order: SVU* and guessing, and this was maybe the first really big operation most of them had been in on. And they were, to a one, kind of dumb.

From: Murder Bimbo
To: Justice Bimbo
October 18 at 1:20PM

Dear Justice,

Honestly, hearing the full plan messed me up. I had known about the basics: that they were going to use me as bait, that I would be the one to kill him. But the details were a mix of insane and boring. First and most shallow, there was no drama to it. Poison? Second, it didn't seem like it was going to work. The other assassination attempt had failed—why did we think we could do better? When we failed, I would surely be fired. This would not be the first job of a long career, it would be a one-off that took me out of sex work long enough to fuck with my protective shell and professional reputation. These guys had acted like I was one of them and I had believed them. It was all fine and good for them to be mediocre white guys. I was the one who had sacrificed one job to get another that was now going to fail miserably.

And if we did fail, would I get arrested? Were they going to set me up to take the fall? I seized in irritation. What was the point of taking a legal job if I could still be arrested for it? It was so crazy, I didn't even think to question it. And why hadn't they covered this fact in their litany of warnings against taking the job?

I needed space to process. I wished I had had a commute to commute, or a friend to call, or someone to fuck. I wished I could go anywhere without worrying about being seen. My future had vaporized, and, weirdly, that wasn't even the worst part. It was the humiliation of believing I'd had a future to begin with.

I went upstairs. I closed the door to my room.

This was September 15. The date was irrelevant to me except as a marker on the way to October 17. I wasn't watching the news or listening to it, and I was barely going out or talking to anyone besides the guys. One by one I saw them leave the house: Walnuts, then Onions, and Eyebrows. I wanted to leave my room, but I wasn't ready to face DC. Just thinking about it forced hot, soundless tears down my cheeks. Then my eyes itched. My nose did, too. I felt like I might hurl and turned on the faucet to cover the sound. Instead, I sobbed. I don't know how long I cried for, but it looked a little darker out when I was done and my cheeks were puffy.

I should leave. I could quit. I could tell them this wasn't what I thought I was getting into. The moment had passed to feign offense. I would have to tell the truth. I had overestimated my abilities. I didn't have the stomach to go through with the murder, and I was really scared of getting arrested. I had taken the job assuming it would be the start of a long career. The sacrifices required were worth it for a long career. But they weren't worth it for a onetime job. Yes, I was used to the risk of arrest in my old job. Not like this, though. *That was totally reasonable*, I thought. Would I get arrested if I quit?

I heard the front door slam and from the window I could see DC jog down the stairs and get into a car. I splashed water on my face and left before I could get stuck crying again or lose my nerve.

No one had told me I couldn't leave the house, but it had been implied. For the plan to work, no one could say they had seen me in the US after I had crossed the border into Canada. I didn't care anymore, though, because I wasn't planning to go through with any of it.

I crossed the street and walked in the opposite direction DC had driven in. It was dinnertime. I passed so many houses with lights on, kids killing time before supper in front of windows or televisions, people coming home from work a little later than they had promised. The moon was out, a few stars. Maybe one of the stars was Mars, I don't know. I kept walking.

I became aware of the people shouting only after I had been walking for twenty minutes or so. This neighborhood was more densely populated than where I'd started, or maybe dinner had ended, but people were out. Second thing I noticed: Meat Neck's name everywhere. Shirts, hats, flags. Anyone who had merch was wearing it. Fuck Meat Neck. Kill Meat Neck. Meat Neck Takes No Shit. Meat Neck for King. I'd Neck Meat. A campaign lawn sign hung duct taped to a stop sign.

Something was up.

Three women stood on a small lawn; two were visibly distressed. They weren't crying, but they were gray and shaky. The third looked like she couldn't figure out which to embrace first. As I got closer she touched one's hand and put her head on the other's shoulder.

I frowned at the comforting woman, like I already knew what was going on in the world.

"This country is fucked," she said, in my direction.

"I've been working all day. What's going on?" I asked. All three women raised their heads like sheep in a pasture.

My directness surprised me—my ignorance surprised all of them.

"It's fucked," the comforter said.

One of the women was opening and closing her mouth, not dramatically, just as if she had lost control of even these few square inches. Her face was dry and her eyes purple-rimmed.

"One of his ex-girlfriends accused him of rape," she said.

"Not when she was his girlfriend." They had heavy Boston accents.

"Not that it matters."

"Not that it matters."

"Not that it matters."

"She said she was never his girlfriend, actually."

"Fuck," I said. Though I'd expected something worse. I had even, for a moment, considered the possibility that he had been killed. My least favorite thing about a crisis is how, within it, seconds unfold into little worlds where alternate realities rise up and fall away, offering impossible, temporary mercy. Not to be too lesbian about it, but at first I didn't really see why they were offended. Everyone knew Meat Neck's reputation. His reputation was for assaulting women in ways that, were it done in a different context, lesbians would have called sex, but straight people called harassment because there was no actual P in V. Was all this outrage because Meat Neck was finally getting caught for rape-rape because he was doing what the straights considered sex-sex?

"That's not the shitty part. He didn't even deny it, he said he *did* do it. And he said he was proud of it. He said we've gotten too soft in this country and that tolerating claims of soft rape—"

"Soft rape."

"Soft!"

"—he said claims of soft rape hurt actual victims."

"And men."

"Yes, he said men first, actually. Men and quote unquote actual victims."

I tried to think of the right thing to say. A motorcycle tore down the street past the house. I jumped. I saw the driver notice. He reached the end of the block, turned around, and came back at me even faster. I tried to stand my ground but my body backed into a bush.

"You're dead, whore," he shouted.

A coincidence. Or maybe just his word for all women. He didn't know me.

One of the women ran to hug me. Her neck was slick with tears and mucus. She pressed me into it.

"It's okay," she said.

I noticed that I was crying, too.

"We are screwed," she said, "we really are."

It's cheesy, I know. I wish I had a better story, but this is real life. These three women who I had never met, who might remember that they met a stranger, but probably couldn't have picked me out of a lineup as soon as I walked away, changed my mind about everything. I thought Meat Neck would be bad for the country, but I hadn't thought he would be effective enough to be catastrophic. But he didn't need to be effective, I realized. There was a violent, angry streak under the skin of the country. All we needed was a leader who celebrated it and it would push to the surface. Scarier than the laws would be what was socially permissible, what was not worth prosecuting, what was not worth stopping.

It shook my body. I understood the weeping. I understood the comforter, too. She was reaching out to these other women not because she was okay but because the quality of her distress was silent, dry, rigid. If he won, we would see every form of distress. We would also see just as many new forms of violence. I knew it wasn't binary, the two would be wrapped up in the same people. They would be expressed every day in events that were impossible to mourn and even harder to analyze. Soon things would grow so twisted that language would have a hard time keeping up. We would grow alienated from each other. How would we ask for help? How would we express love? Bad things happened. But I had always thought the most important thing in the world was not preventing those but creating the conditions needed to repair the harm. How long would those take to wear away?

Not long at all.

And I was in a position to stop it. Me.

It could get me arrested, sure. I could get hurt. I could even get killed, if I was being honest with myself—which was something I hadn't been doing a lot of lately. But I was just one person.

Who was I to decline the responsibility? Who would I be to women, to minoritized people, to all the people Meat Neck would disenfranchise, to all the people who would be the victims of hate from anyone who felt like it? Did I think my life was so much more valuable? What, exactly, was I planning to do with my precious remaining time on earth to make up for *not* doing the single most helpful thing I could in the history of the country?

It was a duty, I realized. It was my duty. This was bigger than me or my career or my lifestyle or any of that. I couldn't walk away.

I would kill Meat Neck.

Again, I was flooded with the same sense of possibility that had started this whole journey. I couldn't see what the future was, but I knew I would be able to one day, and that it would be bright. Suddenly I was able to see the flip side of the stupidity of the guys' plan. They needed me, *me*. I was the one who could transform their silly pieces into an actual, functioning plan. The failed attempts were all just by other dudes like these dudes. I was the missing piece. I had been thinking about it all wrong. I had been trying to be a good employee and follow orders. But really I needed to make sure the plan worked.

So I would do it. I would do it, but after it was done, I would leave. I was not going to take the fall for this. I wouldn't even risk that possibility. Instead of waiting hours with the dead body and leaving with DC, I would leave on my own. I could pick up a rental car, drive out to the country, and take some time until it all cooled off. Then I would regroup.

From: Murder Bimbo
To: Justice Bimbo
October 18 at 2:23PM

Dear Justice,

DC and I took the Amtrak to New York on October 16. We walked separately from Thirty-Fourth Street to the Times Square hotel where he'd booked us rooms.

The rest of the guys came in on their own. Walnuts got a room at the gala hotel and set it up as our control center. We all ate dinner separately and then met him there to run through the plan. I have to admit, I was actually reassured by how professional everyone was being. During the planning I had been overly focused on my own role and on the problems I saw. I hadn't given the guys enough credit for the work they *had* done. There were guarantees and contingencies and backups. Everyone knew their role and took it seriously, but moved with ease.

I had a final moment of wistfulness that I had been recruited into something I would have to leave behind, instead of into a long career as a spy that would somehow end with me being played by Helen Mirren. This would be my last full day. I was actually kind of sad I'd be leaving without saying goodbye, but my exit plan was set.

Morning came. I worked out. I showered. I put on tinted moisturizer, color-correcting cream, mascara, and lipstick. I wore a black sleeveless dress cut almost to my belly button and T-strap Choos with little bows on the front. I flipped my hair into something YouTube called a faux French twist and secured it with a dozen bobby pins. At four, DC and I walked to a boarded-up bodega across from the venue. The rest of the team was inside.

Walnuts handed me an ID on a lanyard, a gala ticket, and an earbud.

"I'll have you on the monitor until you get into the room. Don't worry," Walnuts said.

I must have looked rigid.

"Deep breath," he said. We all took one.

There was a line to get into the hotel, but a tall man with an earpiece motioned me past it.

"VIP," he announced, though my ticket didn't say VIP. Was he also a government agent?

"Bouncer's got a photo database of Meat Neck's personal guests and you're on it," Walnuts said in my ear.

I reflexively covered my ear.

"Don't touch your ear," Walnuts said. I ripped my hand away. No one seemed to notice.

"Good, through the lobby. Meat Neck is in the bar, the bar on the left, eleven o'clock. Take your time. Try not to attract attention," he said.

The hotel was packed with C-list celebrities, men in suits, men in fleece vests with tech logos embroidered on the breast. Everyone looked like the kind of rich people who actually spend their money. They were clustered around high-tops, chatting while checking their phones. The stairs to the mezzanine were flanked with super-sized black cottage cheese tubs. A crypto event sponsored by a men's dairy start-up. Perfect. I didn't recognize the brand. It must have been new. "Massive curds, added fiber," the tubs bragged.

A waiter with a clear acrylic platter offered me a tiny pita chip of tuna tartare with yuzu. I declined. The room was packed. I couldn't have rushed if I wanted to. The sound wasn't overwhelming, but the scents were. As I moved closer to Meat Neck's supposed location I had to pass through a gauntlet of odor pockets: expensive floor cleaner, clashing florals, artificial BO.

I was cataloging these when the crowd split and I saw Meat Neck sitting at the bar, his famously thick lips on a highball. He saw me, too. I smiled. He smiled.

I receded into the lobby. My heart pounded.

"You're good," Walnuts said.

DC approached. I turned toward him. We walked together, to the elevator bank.

The control center was on the fifteenth floor. I was looking forward to seeing Walnuts. I was happy DC was with me. I was shaky, in general, about what I was in the middle of. But it was a good shaky. I felt useful. I thought of the women on the lawn, I thought of Meat Neck's ex-girlfriend and the faces of his allies when they cheered for soft rape. Honestly, I even thought about your wife, Justice. Though I didn't think of her as your wife. I just thought of her as the person who'd risked everything to speak against him. And I thought about myself. I stood up a little straighter. I breathed in deeply and let my body fill with righteousness and courage.

That feeling turned to shit as soon as we opened the control center door.

Walnuts' room was packed with strangers. Men. They were standing in clumps, some were sitting on the beds. Walnuts was at the desk with his computer open next to two other men on their own laptops. There was hardly room to walk. All the men were white. The room smelled like balls. I couldn't put my finger on why, but these guys didn't seem like government operatives.

I turned to DC for comfort, but his face was blank.

"Who are—?" I started.

He shook his head. A few men were leering at me. Most seemed unbothered by our entrance. DC jiggled his head and shook out his jaw. We entered. I moved like a rat trying to avoid the snakes in a box full of snakes. Someone bumped into DC.

"Sorry, bro," the man said. He had ice-blue eyes. He smelled like what I imagine bombs smelled like.

"Looks like everything is going well," DC said.

Walnuts shrugged, like "We're doing our best here."

I counted the men in the room. Twenty-two. The room was very hot. Sweat pooled between my toes. A twenty-third came out of the bathroom. A knock on the door. Twenty-four entered. I watched him. He was wearing a plain black baseball cap and one man seemed to want him to take it off. They argued. I looked around. No one else was wearing a cap. He shook his head, no, he would not remove his hat. Dispute, dispute. Then he lifted the back an inch to show the men what was under it.

What was happening?

That motion, that one inch of scalp, turned a key in my mind on a door I hadn't known was locked, and a new room popped open. I realized I was standing in a different house than I thought I'd been in this whole time. My mouth tasted rotten. I thought I would vomit or faint. Something wasn't just a little wrong, it was very, very wrong.

I scanned the rest of the room and was suddenly, absolutely sure.

Ball Cap had a tattoo on his skull.

Now I noticed Walnuts had one sleeve of his shirt tucked up around his elbow and the other pulled down to the wrist. I had only seen him in long sleeves before. All through the summer, in Boston, he'd kept them long and buttoned.

Over the crest of the collar of a man I'd never seen before, I could see a round black shape.

These men were not government agents. Not the ones in the room, and not the ones I'd been working with.

I could be wrong, I told myself. I tried to find a clue that my analysis was wrong, while trying to find a clue that my analysis was right, while trying to slow down my heart with deep breaths that looked like regular breaths so no one could tell I knew what I thought I knew. I needed another clue. Surely, someone must have been wearing a holster under his jacket, or a badge. If not that, then there had to be evidence of who the men were if they weren't government agents.

Then I caught it. It was a symbol on a patch on a bag mostly tucked under a bed. I swear I'd never seen it before, but it still looked familiar. The only clue I needed. What did it mean? What were the words for what this was?

"Murder Bimbo," Walnuts said, "earth to Murder Bimbo."

I thought, *How long has he been talking to me?* I thought, *Wow "earth to" is a very Gen X expression.* His hand was extended; the pharmaceutical vial was in his palm. My body shook as I went for it. My fingers felt thick and frozen. I told my fingers they were fine, they were graceful, but still I couldn't grip the vial properly and it fell, hard.

I blacked out for a second but did not pass out. I wondered if I had been killed for dropping the poison, but if I had been killed, I thought I probably wouldn't be thinking anymore. Unless this was heaven or hell. But then I was in the hotel room again, learning that there was fear so powerful you could temporarily lose your sight.

"Oops," DC said. He handed me the vial.

I gripped it.

"You sure she's okay?" Walnuts asked.

"I'm fine," I said.

"This isn't too much for you?" he said.

The question converted enough of my fear into anger, and I straightened up. My heart slowed. I swallowed a hard ball of spit.

"Let's go," I said to DC.

"Eighty-eight," I heard one man say to another. Then they looked at me.

The symbol I had seen on the bag, I still couldn't remember the name, it wasn't a swastika or an eagle or one of the common ones, but it was a neo-Nazi thing.

The guys I had spent all summer with were white supremacists. My mind didn't whirl. It was empty. I had a hard time moving my body, so it was good that DC nudged me out the door. If they weren't the government, then when this was all done, the reason we had never talked about after was that there was no after. I wasn't one of them. They were going to kill me. Or the government would. The government which very much wasn't on our side.

Once we were back in the hall, I wanted to be alone so I could figure out what to do next, but there was no time now. My brain was stuck repeating the same fact over and over. I needed it to move on. I needed it to move to the next thought so I could figure out an escape. But I couldn't. Just the same words over and over.

I was working for Nazis.

DC touched my shoulder.

I had stopped walking. We had to keep moving. My body started again, but it felt stalled compared to my rapidly looping mind. We rode down to the lobby, crossed to the opposite side, and got in at a different elevator bank.

Nazis. What was I going to do?

Why did neo-Nazis want Meat Neck dead? Why had they posed as federal agents? Was it just for my sake? It must have helped them get closer to all kinds of people?

DC held out his open palm to me.

"Earbud," DC said. I pulled the thing out of my ear.

"Why pretend to be government?" I said. It surprised me, believe me, that I was reckless enough to ask.

"I told them you were too smart to lie to. Walnuts, you hear that? She figured it out—you owe me fifty dollars," he said.

"Why did you need me?" I said.

"Did? Still do," he said. "This isn't our first attempt. You think that godforsaken Board is the product of the first attempt? Meat Neck always catches on."

"You should have just told me the truth," I said.

Tears were rising. Childish tears.

"Come on, you wouldn't have taken the job. What self-respecting sex worker would work for us?" he said.

He had a point. I knew the kind of people who would have taken the job. The guys were better off with me. They had gotten lucky with me. And they were right: Of course I wouldn't have knowingly worked for neo-Nazis.

Did that change things now? Killing Meat Neck for them was not what I signed up for, but I did think Meat Neck should die. I was in a place to do it. There wasn't a lot of time to get into the details. What would you do, Justice? Don't answer that. I'm guessing you would never get yourself into this situation. But this whole time I thought I had been recruited by the government. Yes, I believed murder was wrong, but I also believed that there were certain circumstances when it might be necessary, and if Meat Neck wasn't one of those situations, I didn't know what was. It was almost funny, the number of times I had given myself little pep talks along the lines of "the Nazis rose to power because the good, quiet people of Germany did not stop them."

You probably want to close this email, delete the whole thread. Nazis are universally evil, and that's the side I found myself on. You have to understand that all of this, all these realizations, came crushing down on me in the space of two minutes, two minutes when I was surrounded by a couple dozen Nazis who were waiting for me to do a job I had agreed to do, and then, probably, kill me.

"You're still in, right?" DC said.

No, I decided, right then. This was a hard line. I couldn't actually kill Meat Neck without understanding why these guys wanted him dead. I couldn't do anything that would put me in league with their politics of hatred. I felt sick. I had to distance myself.

"Yes," I said.

DC needed to leave. I needed him to leave, so I could think through the situation and find a way out. If I left before I went in Meat Neck's room, Walnuts would see. I really didn't want to go in. How long would he be watching the door? Probably at least a few minutes after I went in?

The elevator opened on Meat Neck's floor. DC smiled at me.

"I'll wait until he opens the door," he said.

They're going to kill me, I thought. *The Nazis are either going to kill me or they're going to turn me in for this. Or they will all go down and I will go down, too, as a pro-Nazi traitor. It won't matter who I was before. I was nothing before, after all. That's why they picked me.*

A door a few feet away swung open. Meat Neck. I tried to step toward it but lost my balance and face-planted on the carpet. As I hit the ground, I felt the glass in my bra break, and liquid run down my chest.

"Oh yes," Meat Neck said, "yum."

From: Murder Bimbo
To: Justice Bimbo
October 18 at 3:53PM

Dear Justice,

This next part might be hard to read. Sorry. Trigger warning.

If I'm going to survive, I have to get out of here as fast as possible. I got up. I felt the knee of my tights rip. Meat Neck gave me his hand once I was already standing. It was so soft I wondered if he had a medical condition that made it that way. It felt like a baby's hand. The poison was dripping down my belly.

I went in.

Meat Neck said, "Don't I know you from somewhere?"

I said, "I bet you say that to all the girls."

I had to come up with a way to leave his room quickly. I wished I had brought some Rohypnol or something. I wondered if I could exhaust him (with sex if needed, though I really didn't want to have sex with Meat Neck). I thought about all the nice Nazis who had reassured me it would never come to sex.

But what happened next happened fast.

When you've been in the business as long as I have, you learn to recognize when a man is going to fuck you over. It's rarely one instant. Sometimes it looks like anger, frustration, condescension. Sometimes it looks like a sad kind of resignation as in: I'm so sorry you're making me do this. All of these are normal feelings, it can be hard to tell when they are also a "sign." For Meat Neck it looked like smugness. Like he knew, of the two of us, he was the one doing *me* a favor.

However it happens, my body reacts the same way.

I cry.

"Allergies?" Meat Neck asked.

Tears were streaming down my face.

"I'll just go wash up," I said.

"Wash your cooch, too," he said.

I tried to laugh.

He had stashed a stack of room service trays in the bathroom—had a pile of plates with steak juice on them in various states of congealment. The napkins were untouched. I wondered if he wiped his face at all. I wondered if his fingers tasted like steak. The forks and knives were tucked between plates, making the stacks precarious. That pissed me off. Someone was going to have to lift those stacks.

I unzipped my dress.

The vial had broken into two pieces. I used wet toilet paper to wipe the liquid from my skin and then flushed the last little bit down the toilet.

I heard him calling something close to my name.

I really, really did not want to have to have sex with Meat Neck. I could tell him I forgot something and I'd be right back. It was a dumb thought. It wouldn't work. He wouldn't let me leave. Or he would, but he'd go downstairs. Or he'd call DC to complain. I couldn't sleep with him. I couldn't.

Before I could figure anything else out, he was pounding on the door. The knob turned. He came in. I was undressed to my waist, my left arm restricted by the sleeve.

"I'm ready," he said.

He was shorter than I expected. His shoes were off. He had his hard dick out through the zipper of his suit pants.

"Suck on it," he said.

"Hold on," I said.

"You don't like to suck it?" he said in a half baby voice.

He grabbed my right wrist harder than I thought he was capable of.

"No problemo," he said.

I wanted to remind him that I was there willingly, that I would do what I had been hired for, professionally, very well, that he would not be disappointed. I wanted to make a light joke that set him at ease, probably at my own expense, and then a compliment, then ask him for a drink.

But my throat was dry.

He twisted my arm behind me and pulled up the back of my skirt. He tried to tear off my tights, but he wasn't strong enough for that and had to settle for pulling them down.

"Don't worry, you'll like it like this. You can look at my face in the mirror. I'm going to be the president."

He did rip the crotch of my underwear, but not enough to get through them—he still had to move them to the side.

"See, you like it, see how wet you are, she likes it," he said.

He forced his fingers inside me and pumped a few times. Then he pulled them out.

"Gotta get a condom."

The condom was in his pocket. Unwrapped. For some reason that was the thing that shook me out of frozen panic, thinking of a linty penis. Then I felt his dick push inside me.

"Get off," I said.

"Shhhh, you'll get paid, just got to do the work," he said.

He started pumping.

I needed him to stop.

"Look at my face, do your job," he said. He pumped.

I looked up at the mirror. His lips formed an unnatural wormy rectangle. Whatever he was doing, it hurt, a lot. I winced. He grabbed my hair. The way he held my head, I saw a glint of silver.

Then: pure animal survival. I ripped my left wrist out of my sleeve, and in a move so fast I don't remember it, I grabbed one of the steak knives and plunged it into the soft belly between his ribs and his dick. Then I got him once more in the heart, just to be safe.

ACT II

CLICKING SEND on the final email to Justice is like shedding a fur coat I've swum a mile in. I am relieved to feel my body soften and relax. I need it to. I set the alarm to 7:11 a.m., daybreak. I run water hot enough to turn my hands red and scour my face. I worry I'm too keyed up to get to sleep, but as soon as I close my eyes, I'm out.

When the alarm rings, I am already half-awake, only I didn't know it before the bell. I rub my feet together. I rub my hands on my thighs. I crack my jaw open to yawn. It was the perfect amount of rest. My brain is working again. I heat water for tea. I crack the sliding glass door to the deck and open it wide enough to slip through sideways. The damp wood cools my feet. I look for any sign of people on the property, but it's just my car in the driveway. I go back in the house. I finish my tea.

Now the trek. I find jeans. I find socks. I break a liter of water from a flat pack in the pantry. My go bag is heavier than I remember. The deck is shadowless. Cloud cover. Birds are creaking.

I cross the lawn, pass a shed with a padlock on it, pass a wood pile, then the remains of an old wood pile, then a rusted hunk of metal the size of a tricycle. Then I pass the shed without a padlock on it. I stop to make sure it has everything I'll need later. Yes.

Just a few steps later, I am in the woods.

Within a minute, I can no longer see the house. The path is more challenging than I expected or I'm more tired than I realized. I stumble on roots. If I fall in the woods, I will be bones before anyone finds me, if anyone finds me at all. I try to walk both more quickly and with more care.

I arrive at a steep embankment. This is the frontage road that leads to the highway a few miles up. The first section of the embankment is so steep, I have to take a running start to get up. I need to lay eyes on the road itself.

Sure enough, tire tracks disappear in both directions. It's gravel and overgrown in places, but I'll be able to walk it. I drop my bag at the top of the embankment, where it will be out of sight between a boulder and a log.

I slide down the hill and return to the house as fast as I can. I can see lights in the house from the woods and worry that I have been gone long enough that night has fallen. An impossibility but I still worry. Did I sleep enough? It's still morning. The darkness is just the darkness of the woods. Behind me the leaves shake. Nothing, no one, just wind.

One part is done, now the next.

Have you ever made someone fall in love with you over email? I haven't, but I can. I've done it by text, on apps, purely through emojis on social media. What a high. Some people think digital is less romantic. Fuck, anything can be romantic is my take. As long as your body is in it, if your mind is humming along, if you want it bad enough.

Let's go.

From: Me
To: X
October 19 at 8:41AM

Dear X,

I found a time machine. I took it to the night eight years ago when we were deeply in love, and you invited me for a date on the rooftop rated the third best view of Boston. Even though it was winter, and even though we were both too radical to believe in marriage, I believed you were going to propose and I wore my most diaphanous dress. I had my nails done. I arrived a little early and took a walk around the area so you would have all the time you needed to adjust your suit, to straighten your tie. I wondered if getting married would calm my heart, which reached painfully toward you whenever we were apart. I wondered what our friends would think. I wondered if we would invite our parents. By the time we were supposed to meet, the skin on my legs was numb and I was so excited, I skipped up the steps.

There you were.

I was so disappointed to see you in a baseball cap and jeans that I didn't even notice that you weren't alone.

Half an hour later we walked off that rooftop holding hands, but metaphorically we were already facing different directions. You grew into the person you are now: suits, electric vehicle, wife, every award the Nonprofit Industrial Complex offers for attempting "change from the inside." I split myself in two: anarchist and sex worker. I went harder on both, but never again let one circle of people know I was in the other. You were the last person to see both identities. You were the one who anchored those versions of me together. Without you as a lens, I didn't make sense to anyone, even myself. It is only in writing this that I realize it's really true. What does that mean about how I've spent the last eight years? That is the least of our problems.

The country is worse off than it's ever been, the people are vulnerable. I'm calling you back to the cause. The true left can't afford to have you working so hard for the center anymore. You are too experienced, too persuasive, too fucking good. The center doesn't need you there to fight for their comparative luxuries and put-on indignities. Stop repairing the machinery of a broken system. People are dying without healthcare and housing, people are being deported, violated, arrested.

Until yesterday your mortal enemy, Meat Neck, was poised to inherit the throne. Now he is dead. Maybe you think that's enough. Maybe you think that's such a great start that now you can rest, you can stay where you are. I'm here to tell you: You can't. His death was only the first piece of a bigger movement.

There is a specter haunting America and that specter is anti-fascism. And the church, and the state, and country music, and the Marvel universe have united to decry it/us as a danger to capitalism and the American way. We *are* a danger to capitalism and the American way. It's time to unite. The death of Meat Neck is not a sign that we're doing fine without you. If we are not vigilant, how many zealots will spring up in his place? We need direction. We need help. The job is tailor-made for you. The death of Meat Neck is a welcome-home-to-the-movement gift. I should know. I tailored the job. I made the gift.

I killed him for you.

That night on the rooftop haunts me. Like the people, I need you back. Together we were strong, a singular entity, bound much more tightly than a normal couple. One day the people will remember us as grandmothers of change. I see everything through the vantage of my confidence in us. It is my weakness and my superpower. Sometimes it makes me sad. But sometimes it helps me to see hidden truths. It helps me see when compromises are really capitulations, when libertarians can be context-specific allies, when losses are for the better. I have been biding my time. It took eight years, but finally this power helped me find a moment, an opportunity. Now I'm here to tell you why it means you should come back.

Please keep reading. The truth is, I'm on the lam in a house far from home. It's a miracle no one has come to kill me yet, but somehow I'm still here. I guess, if I die, you'll definitely read these emails. It will be too tempting not to. Maybe then you'll have to come back to the cause in my memory. That would be worth it. My death would be worth your success. That's how important I know you are to the cause.

I hope that doesn't happen, though, and I figure out an escape so we can be together again. But I'm getting distracted.

You'll have to forgive me in advance for sending this in awkward chunks. There is a lot of property where I am. I have to stop often to survey the area, check for cars on the road, any signs of dogs or people. I made a lot of enemies and they all have guns.

I should get to it. I'll say as much as I can before I'm interrupted.

The opportunity. It came as an email. It should have read:

WHITE NATIONALISTS ISO HOOKER TO HELP TAKE DOWN MEAT NECK.

That's not an email. That's a time machine.

Fuck yes, I said, and climbed right in.

From: Me
To: X
October 19 at 9:04AM

Dear X,

Okay, the email did not actually say "WHITE NATIONALISTS ISO HOOKER TO HELP TAKE DOWN MEAT NECK." If it had said "white nationalists," I would have deleted it for racism. If it had said "hooker," I would have deleted it for poor manners. And if it said "take down Meat Neck," I would have screenshotted it, sent it to everyone I knew, and then deleted it because that's insane. What it actually said was a lot more like "ahh, you're so beautiful, I can't believe we live in the same area, I would love to meet and see if we get along. No worries if not." But I am writing this to you from the aftermath, and I'm trying to keep it short but also interesting.

This is a story about strange coalitions—the first of many lessons you drove home when you taught me about effective organizing. I'm writing to you from a luxe getaway–cum-bunker in Vermont. Peak of the leaf-peeping season. The house is so expensive, it looks like there's nothing in it until you start popping open hidden cabinets: gusts of lanolin, tinned fish, the guest ski closet, ebonized walnut millwork, an entire two-story wall of windows in the living room, a steam shower. "Demure" is the word, if a Noguchi coffee table can be demure.

I'm set up in an Eames lounger in a guest bedroom overlooking the mountains, because it is also overlooking the main road to the house. Yes, this is a client's house. Well, he refers to it as his "ski cabin." He's not here. I'm trying to be careful about the mess I make, but it doesn't really matter. There's a man who comes to open the house before the owner uses it. He brings women to clean. They will conceal all history of mess because they are paid to, and because they will be blamed for making it if they don't.

You used to hate it when I texted you from some dude's toilet. You said you weren't jealous about sex work, you were just depressed by it, and these days I am, too. The older you get, the meaner sex work gets, and you start hating everyone or yourself or both—not for the reasons people think you should, just because you're at the intersection of so much human detritus. It's overwhelming. All the "empowerment" is so deeply tied up in unrelenting capitalism and violence. The second lesson you taught me: All work under capitalism is organized for the reproduction of capitalism and the growth of wealth inequality, not toward the well-being of people. Sex work doesn't outsmart the system, it's part of the system, just like every other kind of work.

I started looking for a way out last year (aka researching how to finish my BA, spend a couple years in grad school). I hadn't yet figured it out when I got the email. The guy seemed like an innocuous new client, nice, and a girl has to eat, so I screened him and went.

It was a cool evening after a hot day and people were elated to be outside. My neighborhood smelled like jasmine and burnt Dunkin' with bursts of spent hops whenever someone took out the brewery trash. People shit on Boston, but I still like it.

I crossed through a semipermanent encampment of rich boomers protesting the recent arrest of a local brown homeless man.

"In a way it's a *good* thing he was arrested. If that kind of thing can happen in a place like this, it shows how bad it must be elsewhere, right?" the ringleader had explained the day they'd set up.

"Do you want to say that for TikTok?" I said, holding up my phone.

She didn't know that I was too old for TikTok, or why what she said was fucked-up, but that scared her.

Tonight they seemed to be debating what to do with a chunk of money they'd GoFundMe'd for the homeless man.

"True, we did say it was for bail," one said.

"But as long as it goes to him—like what about if—I mean, we raised it for bail when we were really sure he was innocent," another said.

"Right, I think as long as we give it to him . . ." one said.

Nods all around. I bet they were one minute away from deciding that giving it to a homelessness charity was the same as giving it to the man himself.

They were passing around a Tupperware of Rice Krispie treats while they talked. I was waiting until the ringleader said something even more annoying to tell her the man they arrested wasn't even brown, he was just dark white, but I was going to be late.

The bar was empty. I took a window seat. I ordered a root beer. A toilet flushed and a man waltzed out of the bathroom, gave me a little wave, and sat at the bar. I say "waltzed" because I knew the guy. He'd been stalking me ever since I fired him as my client a few months earlier. I hadn't had a major reason to fire him, I just didn't like him. He had immediately started proving me right. The Stalker swore he would stop stalking me if I just let him hire me again. There's the sex work conundrum in a fucking nutshell. He'd recently started showing up places before I did, which I suspected meant he somehow had access to my texts. Whatever. Not my first stalker, probably not my last. I didn't think he was dangerous, just creepy as fuck, but he was some type of law enforcement, so I hadn't yet threatened him with blackmail or bodily harm.

Two men sat down across from me. Neither was the man in the ID photo the client had sent. But they were definitely there for me.

"We emailed you?" one said.

Right off the bat they seemed gentle, kind. One of them had hair so fair I couldn't stop picturing him sunburned. This was easy because the lower half of his face was covered in cystic acne and whenever he blushed, the skin between the acne turned red, and the whiteheads glowed.

He wore an oversized black tee that read "Ogres Are like Onions." I think that's from *Shrek*. All of this, combined with the fact that he blushed often, made me like him immediately. I started referring to him as **Onions** in my head, to prevent myself from calling him Shrek, which I would have meant affectionately, but calling someone Shrek at a first meeting is a fine line to walk and I didn't want to insult him, even before I knew he was a white supremacist.

The other guy wore basketball shorts. He was a rectangular-headed giant with big soft cheeks and a buzz cut. He wore a silver medical alert bracelet and when he caught me looking he said, "Tree nuts."

"All tree nuts?"

"Not walnuts," he said. He grinned. He was pleased I'd asked. I thought, *This kid wants someone to be his mom.* No problem.

They couldn't have been older than twenty-four.

When I brought up the fake ID, Onions blushed. **Walnuts** apologized. They just seemed so unformed, like two baby moose, clumsy but not malicious. I asked to see their IDs and they handed real ones over.

I should tell you that I happen to know that I've gotten some favorable reviews on the kinds of websites I don't even want to google. I haven't seen these reviews, but I'm guessing they're wherever white power guys go to review hookers and say something like: "really gets it, creamy white queen, five stars, nice tits."

Don't judge. As you know, there are a lot of workers out there who draw a hard line at anything involving race. They'll block you if you even ask. If someone writes to me and says that's what they're into, I block them. But savvy racists don't do that. You tend to find out when you're about ninety minutes into a two-hour date and some small-dicked, especially quiet "accountant" on the brink of blowing his load gets chatty about breeding white babies.

Fine. It doesn't get me off. But work almost never gets me off. That's why they call it work. As long as no one wants me to call them the N word or wants me to role-play slave master, in the moment I'll consider whatever. I'm not necessarily going to rebook those clients, but I am aware that I have a certain clientele who are interested in my whiteness. I would have expected that to bother me, but it just doesn't. You know me, if something doesn't keep me up at night, it doesn't keep me up at night! I charge those guys extra for the race stuff and it's worth it.

This is probably related to my strict barrier between sex work and activism. I know other sex workers incorporate their politics into their work, but it's not for me: (1) I don't want clients to have the first idea about who I really am, and (2) it seems like a slippery slope to thinking all people deserve human touch and adopting a sliding-scale model.

"Look, we don't want to have sex with you," Walnuts said.

"No shit," I said.

They pulled out an envelope with five hundred dollars to cover our hour-long meeting and I was like, okay, sure, I'll meet with you guys anytime, what's the deal.

First they had some questions.

"What do you think of egg dumplings?"

"Fine? I guess?" I said. I had no idea what he was talking about. Onions nodded.

"George Soros?"

"Honestly, I don't know much about him," I said.

Where was this going?

"Does the name Blondi mean anything to you?" Onions said.

That was a band, but that was, if I wasn't mistaken, also Hitler's dog? I didn't know what to say. But they didn't give me a chance anyway. They had more questions.

Would I be willing to help entrap someone? Would I be willing to film videos with a prominent man to discredit him?

At this point, I was thumbing the cash and thinking this would make an interesting story, but I was out, because whoever these skinheads wanted to frame was probably not someone I wanted to frame.

But they kept going. Would I be willing to get this guy to the right spot so someone could beat him up? What if it was a guy who I hated?

"Sure, sure, sure, sure," I said. "But listen, guys, not to yuck your yum/no judgments, but maybe you better give me an idea of who this guy is, because I don't know what you read about me, but we may not be a hundred percent aligned on who we hate, so."

And these guys looked at each other like hungry weasels deliberating.

My phone buzzed. Text from an unknown number.

You owe me!

Who the fuck is this? I typed.

I glanced back at the guys, who seemed to be having an entire conversation in a series of looks.

"Tell me," I said.

"What about Meat Neck?" one said.

"I'd kill that motherfucker myself," I said.

From: Me
To: X
October 19 at 9:52AM

Dear X,

Tiny bit of context: Another reason I said sex work sucks is that I'd recently gotten entangled with a very pretty girl who identified as a "luxury experience curator." We met at a party and in a tipsy haze I told her to call me if she ever needed someone "like me." I had woken up the next morning with a handful of texts from her calling me "bella," and realized that no matter how pretty she was, she was definitely full of shit. I snoozed her attempts to book me. But I didn't cut her off. My fake reason for not blocking her was because boundaries hadn't worked with the Stalker, so why enforce them again? My real reason was I didn't want to, because she was so pretty.

The Curator had four major marks against her. The first: She claimed she was on a $150,000 retainer with a sheikh. The second was that if this was true, she was dangerous, and if this wasn't true, she was really annoying. And the third was that she was the most charming person I had ever met. If I were a sheikh with an extra $150,000 a year, I would give it to her. So the fourth mark against her was actually a mark against me. I had dangerously mixed feelings about the Curator. Have I mentioned how pretty she was?

I'm thinking of taking a break from work, but I can do it this one time, I said, the next time she texted. I assumed I would have to endure one medium cat who thought he was a fat cat for less than I usually make, as a favor to a pretty girl/to pay off my snooze bill.

Fab, she wrote back. She sounded so friendly, cute even.

I went to a hotel downtown where she had procured a pile of ketamine and set up a twenty-person "sex party" of many queer genders that was designed to seem like an organic, fun time but was really a well-orchestrated machine for one foreign centimillionaire who wanted to feel like all the cool kids wanted to fuck him. I was mostly there to round out the crowd and spent the evening fisting an anime amalgam in a green-and-pink wig for maybe the easiest two grand I had ever made.

I left thinking I might have judged the Curator too soon. I agreed to show up the following week for a "similar event," which turned out to be similar only in that the drugs were white and the man was a foreign centimillionaire and there was more than one woman of more than one gender. But instead of getting to fist a sexy cartoon girl, I had to do some really debasing stuff with a woman who looked underage or underfed and who spoke no English.

So that night, in the bar, sitting across from Onions and Walnuts, when I got a text from an unknown number, I replied Who the fuck is this? What I got back was a headshot of the Curator.

You know her??

I didn't know what to say.

She works for me, you owe me $2800.

Next time you're late, there is a penalty.

I got a literal cold sweat. I took a screenshot of the threat and sent it to the Curator.

Lol omg

Then, a second later.

I'll take care of her, don't worry. It's nothing.

I did worry. I ordered tequila.

The guys clarified that they did not want to kill Meat Neck. I winked and said "I know." We chatted. But I really was curious about their motivations. Eventually I had the right number of drinks to rub away the thin film of decency that prevented me from asking.

"Not to paint you all with a broad brush but I'm surprised YOU guys want to kill Meat Neck," I said.

The one who had also, apparently, passed decency said, "Because he's a motherfucker!"

We all laughed.

Then the other one said, "It's part of a bigger thing, a bigger, like, a grander what's it called."

Reich, I didn't say.

"Plan," I said.

"PLAN!" Walnuts shouted.

"So how much will you pay me?"

"That depends," Walnuts said.

"Five hundred thousand," Onions said.

Half a million dollars. And that was their initial offer, which I knew meant they had more.

I don't need to tell you how much I love money. I like to spend it, but I love to have it. I wish I could Scrooge McDuck into a pool of gold. This remains my embarrassing vice, the bruise on my Marxist cred. I've stopped trying to figure out whether it's a contradiction to my politics or just a symptom of capitalism's pernicious fingers in my psyche. I just like it. Sometimes I try to make myself feel better by imagining how I would redistribute my wealth, or the amount of good, necessary shit I could fund. There's a role for a pool of gold in the revolution!

I remember you told me you thought that one day I'd make a million dollars. I don't know what you meant by that, but at the time, it was such a beautiful thought that all I could imagine it meant was that one day you thought I'd make a million dollars. Later, when we were falling out, you cited money again. You accused me of being blinded by my desire for it. I accused you of wanting to be with someone financially stable yet somehow also radical.

Walnuts conceded, yes, they had $500,000 to pay me. I didn't press them about "for what" at that moment. It seemed like the answer was either to flirt with Meat Neck or to meet with him or to alert someone else to his whereabouts and to possibly be in a sex tape.

I knew this would be a route back to you, a chance to redeem myself in your eyes. But maybe more immediate to me was the fact that it would be a chance for retribution for what Meat Neck did to me personally, which I'm sure as fuck not going to waste time rehashing here.

Maybe it's weak that I'm more compelled by my personal victimization or a second chance at love. When the possibility of eliminating Meat Neck for the rest of the world should be motive enough. But actually what does it matter? All the reasons are good.

Usually when something bad happens to you, it leaves a wound that slows you down or inhibits your life or just really fucking annoys you. Or it becomes a scar that maybe doesn't hurt anymore, but every time you look at it, you remember what happened. When you met me, I think I was still in shock. I hadn't let the fact of what happened into my consciousness yet. But then I did.

Over the last eight years, what Meat Neck did to me has transformed into pure instinct. Whenever his name is said, my brain is hijacked and I'm steered toward destruction. So I would describe my feelings toward Meat Neck at the time of this meeting as electric, homicidal attraction. I hadn't been face-to-face with him in over a decade and I was ready for another shot. Plus, I figured, this was my way out of sex work! The fabled one last job where I risk it all for the big win.

Still, I wasn't about to take the first offer.

"A million," I said.

Onions' mouth fell open. He looked like a little kid.

"That's fine," Walnuts said. He barely shrugged.

Onions tried to close his mouth so slowly it would be imperceptible.

"What's next?" I said.

"Come over to our house," Walnuts said.

"Not tonight," I said.

Walnuts laughed.

"Of course not tonight! Why would you come tonight!" Onions shouted. Onions laughed. I didn't know why they were laughing, but I started laughing, and I found out, because I could feel it, too. We were laughing because it was funny.

From: Me
To: X
October 19 at 10:28AM

Dear X,

It really is so fucking pretty here. I tried to write to you from the living room. I pushed the sliding glass door open and sat in one corner of the massive U-shaped sectional, tucked my feet under me, and turned toward the wall of windows. But the red and yellow leaves fluttered so gently, so consistently, it was irresistible. I started to watch them, and after a few minutes I must have fallen asleep.

I woke to a smooth, low rumbling sound I couldn't place. I was so disoriented that for a second I wondered if my eyes were still closed, if I was dreaming. But I touched them, and they were open. The sound was coming from the windows. A giant automated shade was slowly lowering. It must have responded to the sun or maybe it's on a timer. I watched as it extended to halfway down the glass before it stopped. I shook out my jaw.

The guy who owns the house gave me permission to use it anytime. That's the kind of things clients do when they're at their most besotted—or maybe he's just constitutionally generous. He's a sixty-five-year-old lawyer who likes vanilla sex and New Wave music. Granted, this was a few years ago, so I was surprised the code at the gate was still the same. It's more likely that he forgot he gave it to me than that he kept his promise. Despite how rich he is, he's stupidly lax about security, which isn't ideal for my current situation.

It's a problem that I let myself get relaxed enough to fall asleep. That gate isn't going to stop a professional, and the walls that extend from it don't come close to enclosing the whole property, so I'm basically a sitting duck inside a house that looks like it was built by AI trained on old issues of *Dwell* magazine and prompted with "world-class mid-century modern."

I walked the property when I got here, located all the entrances, determined the best escape routes and hiding spots. I checked all the locks and latches to make sure they were closed but that I could open them quickly if I needed to get out. I keep my shoes on.

But who am I kidding? I'm not expecting to be slowly stalked or encircled by a team. I'm alone out here and it's not like they gave me assassin training. All it would take is a guy with a gun, maybe two.

Sorry, I guess I should acknowledge that I know we haven't spoken in forever and I'm not sure if you'll read this. If you opened it, though, you're probably reading it. So, hi. I've written and deleted so many explanations, apologetic decision trees, pleas. I even considered playing innocent—telling you that this whole thing is totally aboveboard, that I'm over you, and you're just an erstwhile political ally to me. But you're not going to believe that because it's not fucking true.

I checked the lesbian bylaws. National crises, local severe weather events, and hyper-specific and personally pertinent news stories are the conditions under which it is legal to text your ex. And so I reach out as if with a prodding foot across the bed in the middle of the night. Are you still there? I'm still here.

Okay, turns out it is bizarre writing you like this. Even if it is, by chance, okay with you, I forgot it might not be okay with me. It's waking up parts of my body I haven't felt in a long time. Oops.

You were right about how sad it feels to be the smartest person in the room.

"Come to me when you fucking get it," you said, in anger, at the end, more than once.

I knew that was a sarcastic dig, but I didn't understand the rest of it. I didn't understand how profoundly lonely it can be to be, well, smarter than everyone else. Now I know you actually meant please, really, come to me when you fucking get it. Of course, I know you assumed I never would—not out of judgment of me but out of a deep belief in the intractability of your own loneliness.

I didn't understand, because I had never been as lonely as you had at your worst moment. Obviously, that was arbitrary. I had been just as alone. After my family disowned me and I had to leave college, I should have been suicidally sad, but I wasn't. After my family came back and I thought they loved me, but then found out they had told everyone I was a drug addict, I should have been lonely, but I was just mad. You helped me understand that just because they were working-class didn't mean I should give them the benefit of the doubt or forgive their bigotry. You helped me to see I had that strength inside me before I could see it myself. And on the days when I feel sad about them, I still remember that it was you who told me that was okay and normal. You can feel grief for people without needing to reconnect with them.

You're my witness, too. You know I always clean up the story of my past a bit for the audience, so I don't get pigeonholed as a tragic figure. It's hard to be a sex worker from alcoholic, abusive parents who disown you for being gay. It's so cliché! You've heard me tell the toned-down version so many times and nodded along. Thanks for being the person who knows it's so much worse than what I tell everyone else. It helps me remember the truth.

I'm so grateful to you for that. For all of that. I wasn't grateful enough when we were together, because I didn't see it. I never felt as lonely as I could have when things were bad, because you were there with me. And I never felt as lonely as I could have when things were great because, honestly, they were only great because of you. I hadn't yet figured out how to make my life great by myself.

But here I am. I get it. It's hard to be alone when you're sad, but fuck, it's lonely to be at the top of your game with no one to love.

After I killed Meat Neck, I so badly wanted to come home to you. I wanted to fall asleep on your couch, to wake up the next day and not talk, just walk around together and do whatever errands. It was like he was a balloon that had been inflated between us, bigger and bigger for years. And now that he popped, we fall side by side. In this fantasy we don't *need* to talk about it, because you know everything by osmosis.

I know you're not beholden to me. Just because you're the only person who *can* understand doesn't mean you owe me that. Just because you're the only cure for my loneliness, well—loneliness isn't deadly.

What I'm trying to say is, I miss you.

From: Me
To: X
October 19 at 11:01AM

Dear X,

It was a no-brainer saying yes to the guys. I didn't know if they had a shot in hell of succeeding, but I knew right away I was going to do everything I could to see that they did. I wrote down the address and traipsed back home, past the neighbors' consciousness-raising folding table.

The room spun. I drank a glass of water. I closed my eyes, and it got worse. I opened them, and it got worse again. I was stuck in an infinity mirror of drunkenness. How many tequilas had I had? A double after I got the text message, a double to cheers the deal. One more, to keep the laughter going. Still diffuse, but shouting at me from somewhere I couldn't see, was the idea that this scheme might be a second chance with you, the opportunity to fix what I messed up all those years ago. After all, in a way, it was Meat Neck who came between us. Maybe Meat Neck could bring you back.

The next morning, I dragged myself to the three-story duplex with drop ceilings where the guys had set up shop. Onions waved me in. He was unloading flat packs of IKEA onto the porch. I didn't expect much from the guys in terms of organizing skills and they didn't disappoint. Walnuts took me upstairs. It smelled like banana vape fluid. There were five guys altogether. A man with a line shaved in his eyebrow was prying open a window that had been painted shut. *Fucking landlords*, I didn't say, because the first rule of coalition building is observe and learn, and so far **Eyebrows** was only cursing his own fingernail strength.

The last two guys were in the kitchen, screwing together barstools. One of them had a sharp, buoyant Adam's apple and thick white sneakers, which, combined, made him seem about seventeen years old. He was twenty-one, I told myself, because seventeen gave me ethical pause. Helping **17** was the only guy in the place who looked like he might know what the fuck he was doing. Whether he was actually more competent or just older, more relaxed, and more dorkily dressed remained to be seen. He took off a long-sleeve tee, under which he was wearing a faded black T-shirt with Batman's Penguin on it. Comic books. That figured. In my head I called him **DC**.

I had a flashback to some organizing you and I did with Showing Up for Racial Justice when we were together. I was young and worried about misogyny from the men, homophobia from the older women, miscellaneous respectability politics from the boomers.

"'Coalition' is a magic word," you told me, "it's how you bracket everything and get to work."

It didn't matter that we were on opposite sides of everything else.

I found a butter knife for Eyebrows and shook hands with the rest.

For the first few days we organized our workspace. We built furniture and stocked the fridge, brought in whiteboards and a giant table Onions found on the side of the road, where we laid out all our research and equipment. I realized why office team-building exercises are often based on solving real-world problems unrelated to the job with a coworker. We developed a patter. I started to feel like the guys were my friends. Or, not my friends but my dumb little brothers. They made a game out of trying to get me to laugh. DC mostly stayed out of it, like a polite my-age brother, and together we developed a cute family rapport where they were the jokesters and DC and I were their adoring and much-smarter audience.

When we ran out of boxes to flatten and trash to take out, everyone stalled.

"Okay, so why don't you guys give me the background, catch me up," I tried.

They went over the basic idea: We were going to make a sex tape with Meat Neck as the star and distribute it to discredit him, because they were so red-pilled, they believed Meat Neck was actually a puppet of the Silicon Valley tech billionaires who would be elected to office on the backs of the white working class only to suddenly have a "woke epiphany," change parties, and act with the speed of an authoritarian leader to advance radical left causes and destroy civilization as we know it. I did not bother arguing with them about how insane and improbable this was, both because it was working in my favor and because I was entertained by the fact that they were actually so close to hitting on the truth, while believing in its complete opposite. I wanted to discredit Meat Neck because I thought he was exactly the kind of evil he purported to be.

Walnuts had physically written a list of the things that needed to get sorted out. I couldn't see what was on it. I felt it was my role to keep spirits high for some reason. Probably internalized misogyny.

"Sounds great. Let's get down to details," I said.

"Right, time to focus," Walnuts said.

"'Focus' is a weird word," said Onions.

"FOLK us," said Eyebrows.

"Focus focus focus," said Onions.

"I'm serious," said Walnuts.

"Foooks," said DC.

Onions frowned benevolently.

"That doesn't even make sense," said Eyebrows.

DC looked a little sad. I chucked him on the shoulder. He smiled. It felt good, the whole series of events, because it felt like we were practicing getting something done, even if that thing was just failing at a joke and getting over it.

"Okay, for real, what's first?" Onions said.

"Location," said Walnuts.

Silence.

"Where to record the tape," Walnuts said.

The guys cast looks around the room, like the room might help. Looks at the floor, looks out the window, closed eyes as if the answer would pop into the blank field of their heads.

"Low kate shun," said Eyebrows.

We spent maybe ten minutes talking, just repeating the same pattern:

problem, silence, joke, insult, silence, topic change. I came to understand the piece of paper probably said who, what, where, when, how. I stepped in.

"Can I take notes?" I said, reaching for the paper.

"Yeah!" more than one said. But Walnuts didn't give me the list; he crumpled it into his pocket.

"Not on this, this has other stuff on it," he said.

"Your crypto key?" I said.

Eyebrows laughed. Walnuts did not.

Onions was twisting in his seat, Walnuts was tapping his foot, 17 had been staring at his phone for a while.

"Let's break for lunch," I said.

Onions leaped from his seat, but it was 17 who was out the door first. DC and I were left alone.

"That went well," he said.

"This one's on us. How old are these guys, fifteen? What did we think we were getting into?" I said.

DC laughed.

From: Me
To: X
October 19 at 12:10PM

Dear X,

It took a few days to develop a process, but then we started planning. There were hundreds of pieces to figure out. And that's how they felt, like pieces. Maybe that's because we didn't have a leader to turn the work into a coherent narrative. I don't know. We just noticed problems and tried to fix them. Some pieces were huge and some were tiny, and the hardest part was switching between them without losing concentration. Well, maybe that was the second-hardest part. The first-hardest part was that the guys preferred baroque solutions. They vamped too much. They loved to float ideas they had no practical means to achieve.

They had all been identified as prodigies at some point. Maybe some of them had earned this label with effort and talent. If so, they had since stopped worrying too much about effort and were coasting on other peoples' memory that they could do things. And some of them, I suspected, had been called prodigies because they were men capable of outwitting other men with their thought experiments and therefore considered "promising." All of them were a little "too smart" to worry about whether they were effective at their jobs. They were at the stage in their careers where they just needed to look busy, arguably make an effort, and wait to get a little older until they could be seen as Ideas Guys.

Their ineptitude made work a slog, but that was fine. That was good even. If I'm being honest it felt like the hairshirt I deserved. Eight years ago, you gave me a chance to do things the easy way and in my naivete I said no. It was only fitting that this time through would be littered with inept Nazis constantly questioning and undoing my work.

The exception to the team's ineptitude was DC. DC understood that the measure of good work is whether the job gets done rather than looking busy. Like me, he was there to achieve something. DC and I launched a covert op within a covert op to make sure the mission worked, without anyone ever knowing. The closer we got, the more confused I was about how he had gotten linked up with this crew. He continued to seem a little too normal and a little too competent to fit in. But I didn't linger on trying to figure it out. We all had different motives, and, as I've said, motives were beside the point.

Our first real work was identifying an opportunity to get Meat Neck alone. Meeting him in his home would have reduced the risk of getting caught by an outsider, but it would make me the most vulnerable in the moment and would have required the most travel since he didn't have a place in the Northeast. Luring him to a location of our own felt impossible. Meat Neck was famously impulsive and often seemed to decide what to do based solely on rejecting others' plans for him. We had to get someplace we knew he would already be.

After a few weeks of reading campaign newsletters, tabloids, and private jet Reddit, we were running short on ideas. 17 got frustrated, Walnuts sullen. Eyebrows said maybe we should all take a day off.

"Or a couple of days," Eyebrows said when no one perked up.

"Let's take lunch," DC said. "I have an idea."

When we came back DC put a case of PBR on the table.

"What's this?" I said.

"Beer," 17 said.

My head rocked so far back on my neck I almost hit it on the couch.

"We can all see it's beer," Onions said.

"I got his schedule," DC said.

"What?" I said.

"Dude, yeah!" said Onions. The guys stood. The guys high-fived. The guys cracked beers while, just for one second, I suspected foul play. Just when things had felt hopeless, DC had accomplished something that had been previously impossible. It smelled off.

"Where did you get it?" I said.

"Does it matter?" DC said.

"No," said Onions.

"By any means necessary, that's Machiavelli," said Eyebrows.

"I don't think that's Machiavelli," I said.

"I know Machiavelli," he said.

"Maybe it *is* Machiavelli," DC said. That made me laugh, and the laugh reminded me that I liked DC, and that everyone in on this operation was totally shady to begin with.

This was my coalition! I let it go.

DC started reading through all the events on Meat Neck's schedule, assessing them. Sporting events were out. Political events might draw bigger names, who came with bigger security. Parties were best, we thought, because they wouldn't be as tightly controlled as dinners or other small private events. We agreed on a gala in New York in October because it was far enough away that we had time to plan.

One thing we worried about a lot was that Meat Neck would claim the sex tape was a fake.

"How can we prove it's not?" I said.

"We have to get you on the security footage," Walnuts said, "as much as possible."

"We need to figure out what kind of security they'll have," I said.

"I can get us the hotel layout with CCTV indicated," DC said. Again, I didn't ask him how. I told myself he could get the CCTV layout the same way I would have been able to say "I can get him to take his pants off." We moved on to the specifics of the sex tape.

Maybe sex work had jaded me, but I really couldn't come up with something. Eyebrows believed it was just a matter of finding a disgusting-enough sex act.

"Like pee?" 17 said.

"No," said Eyebrows.

"Like BDSM stuff?" said 17.

"Nooo," said Eyebrows.

His eyes gleamed. His mouth watered. It was clear he was thinking of something very specific.

17 kept guessing. The rest of us left him alone with his fantasies.

"I'll work on a connection with Meat Neck," I said.

"What? No, we can handle that," said Walnuts.

"It's okay, I don't mind. I'm not doing anything," I said.

"I did it," Walnuts said.

"Oh, you did?"

I believed him for a second.

"I'm going to. I know how," he said.

"Okay, well, let me just take one more thing? Anything you guys want," I said.

"Cameras?" DC said.

"Yo, that's part of surveillance," Onions said.

"No, it's a separate thing. The device you use to make the tape is different from the one you use to make sure the route is clear," DC said.

"Okay, sure," Onions said.

I rewatched season four of *Desperate Housewives* on silent because I'd already figured out what we should use to make the sex tape. I would feed the information to them later and make it seem like their own idea.

I'm compressing our work, so it sounds like it took an afternoon, because it makes a better story, but in reality, we did eight- or nine-hour days four or five days a week. We started at twelve and always broke for takeout for dinner.

The project seemed to be the guys' only real interest in life besides spending money. They had a lot of money coming in, so there were always new boxes around: sneakers, gaming stuff, protein bars, supplements. They gave me cash as if it were leftover change in their pockets at the end of the day. Sometimes I went home with a few twenties, but more often it was a few hundred or a thousand. None of this counted toward what they owed me for the job, which was slated to hit my account in two big payments on the day we made the tape and the day the tape was released.

For weeks, DC and I were busy. We learned security protocols and read about code names that ultimately didn't help with anything. We tested the cameras, and I practiced placing them discreetly. 17 tried to teach me sleight-of-hand tricks that might help if I needed to set up cameras while Meat Neck was staring right at me. There were so many pieces to put together: Once we had the tape, we needed to make sure it looked good enough, but not edited. Then we had to get it out to people, people who would trust what they saw and who other people would then trust to report on it.

I was energized and happy. You know how we always used to make fun of that saying "If you do something you love, you'll never work a day in your life"? Well, I spent that first few weeks kind of making fun of us for that, because it was true. Then, when the sheer novelty and the initial endorphin rush that comes with wads of cash wore off, I was surprised to find an even better feeling settle in. I felt confident, adept, well-suited for what I was doing. My talents, my expertise, even my temperament were coming together into a new vocation! The symmetry of it, the fact that the act was also comeuppance, was delicious. Meat Neck had attacked me when I was young and strong, and he was weak. Now he was a legend, but soon I would be, too.

Are you anxious, reading this, wondering whether he would ultimately recognize me? Looking back on it, I'm a little surprised I wasn't obsessing over that question. I thought about it from time to time, but I just intuited that it wasn't going to be a problem. If he brought it up I thought I could tell him he was wrong, or that I'd met him in a different context, or even that he was right and that I was excited to see him again. I guess I felt so sure that what he had done to me hadn't registered to him as abundantly evil that I didn't think he would avoid me. I definitely didn't think he'd be scared of me. And that was the key to getting to a man like this: You had to be someone he wouldn't dream of being afraid of.

I put money aside for rent and utilities, I caught up on doctor visits, then

I bought new sneakers, new clothes, and two new computers, and upgraded my phone. Then I just started tucking the cash away. One day I got home with three grand in my pocket and realized I had almost $40,000 tucked into various books in my apartment.

I decided I needed to get seriously organized. I didn't know how severely we'd be punished if we were caught releasing a sex tape. But I knew enough about how wealth in America works to know that when we were done, I would need a safe (non-extradition) place to retreat. My face would be on the video. There would be no getting out of my association with the crime. But, and this might be crazy, it seemed possible to me that I could become sort of a folk hero to people, if the plan worked. I could see T-shirts with my face, some kind of catchy slogan. Then again, could I achieve icon status if people knew I had knowingly colluded with Nazis? TBD. Whatever else, I knew I needed a plan. On days I didn't go to Somerville, I started figuring out how to disappear.

Before I looked into it, I thought it would be hard to find a way out of the country without leaving a trail for the feds. It's not. One word: Reddit.

From: Me
To: X
October 19 at 1:14PM

Dear X,

It's my favorite part of the day. One p.m. Most people are just starting to become productive, and I've already had a whole day. It's misty here. I didn't know Vermont was misty and warm in October. I desperately want to go out on the deck to be closer to the mountains, to feel the strange wet warmth on my skin, but it's not a good idea.

The longer I'm here, the higher the likelihood that someone is going to show up. When that happens, I don't want to be on a deck without easy escape routes. I want to be in the center of the house, invisible to anyone approaching, able to pivot toward any of my planned exits with ease. Action feels imminent, which is making me emo.

Oh, also, I'm drinking espresso. I made myself an espresso. You taught me about espresso. I wish I could make you one, too.

You're the one who instilled fairness in me, nuanced, real fairness. You instilled it so that it would roll around like a pebble in my shoe.

We met on the dance floor. Remember? Your girlfriend didn't want to dance and mine did, but only as a joke. When I had to go home with mine it felt like my skin was a shrinking sheath trying to squeeze me into the ozone. The next night, when we had accomplished the magic of getting each other's names and numbers, and getting in touch and setting up a secret date, then preparing for that date, and traveling to the cold edge of the Charles River, we agreed there was nothing wrong with how we'd met, but that we would break up with our girlfriends, forward date our anniversary a couple of weeks, and tell everyone we met online. We believed it was true because it might as well have been.

We made a life together far better than either of us expected. On this we always agreed. We moved into a new apartment. You said we had all the good parts of marriage. We weren't just two people, we were me and you and us together, a third thing, with different skills and strengths than we had apart. We developed our own vernacular, which made it expedient to process everything that happened to us. I was always interested in your perspective, and you were constantly astonished, you said, by my depth of feeling. There was never that numbness I get so often when I've outpaced someone in conversation and have to decide whether to change the topic to something we can both play with or just give up. Once I caught up to your reading, I think you felt the same way.

What you taught me, or encouraged me to teach myself, was a whole world of theory. You translated language I thought was too complicated. I was afraid of using words I didn't fully understand, phrases from Marxists, critical race theorists, psychoanalytic writers, feminist scholars, queer theorists. You showed me that none of the terms were unnecessarily complex, none were meant to be exclusionary. It was the opposite. They were big, intricate phrases for big, intricate concepts. They captured multivalent ambivalences, intersecting oppressions, cognitive dissonances. Once you knew how to use them, you could move big ideas around, negotiate with them, explain your circumstance, make sense of a violent world.

The best part of our shared language was not even that we could move through the world together like this but that we really saw each other, and loved each other. Being able to witness the world around us together, on the same level, I've never had that with anyone else. I don't think you have, either. Instead of going around in a constant muddle of frustration or having to switch focus between what's around and who you're with, it's all the same train of thought.

We had a quiet life. Understanding ourselves and our struggles in context afforded us that. I worked at the café and did sex work and read everything you gave me and more. We did Food Not Bombs, collected mutual aid, tried to be good neighbors and thorns in the side of the state. We talked about how if we were born a little earlier and in Ireland we would have joined the IRA. You said thank God you hadn't become an ecoterrorist in college like you wanted to, because then you would have been in jail, and we never would have met. You shared with me your personal quest against violent men and described it in a way that didn't implicate sex work or me or make me feel bad. I learned how it felt when love took a different form than pleasure.

You helped me recognize and heal from my childhood crap. You helped me realize it was crap at all! Until I met you, I felt it was just a natural distance between my parents and me. We weren't best friends, and they didn't kill themselves trying to use the right language for me and my queer friends, but they had always been kind to my girlfriends. They gave me a safe home until I left for college. They tried to send me presents and offered me flights home I knew they couldn't afford. But when they met you, I saw the side of them I had been in denial about.

We took them out to eat and they asked you about your name more than once. Was it real, they wanted to know? You were too tough for that to actually hurt your feelings, but the fact that they could have hurt your feelings should have been enough, you said, for me to feel disrespected by them. And you were right. I started to see all their microaggressions. The more I pointed them out, the more my mother argued I was being impossible. That did hurt my feelings. You helped me establish boundaries and eventually go no-contact. Helped me really understand the clutch heteronormativity has on most families, and the way it made me feel beholden to people who didn't really see me, and therefore couldn't really love me.

It was such a relief to me that you had dated sex workers before when we met. There were so many things I didn't need to define (or defend). And you were gentle about it, caring for me after work in ways that no one else had ever thought to. You made me smoothies and stayed awake with me. You snuggled up and watched movies. You understood when I told you about the standard levels of violence or abuse I encountered. You calibrated your feelings to my own.

But we kept sex work in a container. When we talked about sex work, we talked only about sex work. You weren't sensitive, but still I was careful to do my part to limit the topic. Until the day we were out to eat and you first mentioned your hatred of a minor politician named Meat Neck.

"Oh, I know him," I blurted.

It was five p.m. and we were the first to order dinner at your friend's restaurant. You turned red. I turned red because I had turned you red.

"Sorry," I said.

"No, it's okay. How?" you said.

We were at the bar. The bartender was listening.

"Work," I said.

"Not surprised," you said.

I didn't know what to say next. We sipped our drinks. I had already told you about a client who had done unspeakable things to me, a client I had refused to see again, not because he was dangerous, really, but because of how shitty he had made me feel about having a body at all. "What do you think danger means?" you had asked me then. And I knew you loved me more than I loved myself, and I loved you harder for that. *Teach me how to love myself*, I wanted to beg.

As we sat at that bar, I tried to create a psychic barrier of some kind that would prevent you from putting together that Meat Neck *was* the client. But I had already said too much. You were silent until the bill came. I chattered. You picked up the check. You never picked up the check because I made so much more money than you did. You were in grad school. I had had two drinks and an expensive entrée. I felt so guilty.

I thought you would raise the subject of Meat Neck when we left the restaurant, but you didn't. Then the fact that you didn't mention it became the next piece of proof that you knew. I felt like I was committing a second crime by not bringing it up. I could see something was making you feel bad and I wasn't addressing it. Second crime, because as soon as you responded the way you did, the thing Meat Neck had done to me felt like a first crime that I had committed. His crime against me somehow became my crime against you. And I was sorry. I was so sorry. I didn't know how to make it better.

You raised the topic a couple of weeks later.

We had just come home from our first-anniversary trip to Puerto Rico.

I was boiling water for pasta. You were chopping mushrooms and dill. It was just a little too cold outside to eat on the stoop. We had been discussing what movie to watch later. You told me there was something serious you wanted to talk about. I needed to hear you out.

"You should come forward," you said.

This was the first time either of us had acknowledged that the bad client was Meat Neck, and we both knew without having to say it directly.

"No," I said. It was a reflex. You made your "my feelings are hurt" face, which, despite your insistence it was about hurt, always looked like anger to me. I absolutely panicked.

"I'm sorry, tell me what you mean," I said.

"The system is obviously fucked-up. It's not like he's going to be arrested, but if he did that to you, don't you think he's done it to other women? Or he will," you said.

The oldest argument in the book. Why was it my responsibility to hurt myself more in order to possibly protect other women? Why does so much of the burden to stop harm fall on women? Especially when we both knew I probably wouldn't be successful. Much more respected women had gone up against much less powerful men and been destroyed—women with college degrees, real jobs, lawyers. The system chewed them up and spit them out. And yet victims were still supposed to sacrifice everything in the hopes that they might slow down a predator's violence, even if it was only by leaving a residue that might one day thicken enough to make a difference or, better yet, incidentally hitting on the exact right cultural moment that it would actually work to take him down, only to become the exception that proved the rule.

"Normally, you'd be right," you said.

But Meat Neck wasn't a normal case. Meat Neck was a monster on another level, at least that's the trajectory he was on. If he could possibly be brought down now, didn't we have to try?

It wasn't we, though, it was me. And I was scared.

"I'll never work again," I said. It was the least of my worries, but the only one I could say aloud. I am still kicking myself for that.

"Would that be so bad?" you said. I knew that even though you supported me day to day, you believed sex work was an inevitable by-product of patriarchy and, therefore, fundamentally bad. I still loved sex work then, believed it was good and good for me. It was fun, it was interesting, I had more control over my time and body than people do in most jobs.

I saw the path out of the fight you wanted to be in—it was a fight about how you didn't understand or respect sex work after all. I guided you toward it and you dropped Meat Neck altogether.

Months went by.

You raised it again. My panic didn't return this time, but the idea made me tired. I was preemptively tired by all the talking I would have to do. I didn't think anything would happen if I came forward, and I couldn't imagine doing so much work for nothing.

You called me lazy, which I conceded, because I was. You let it go.

When the lawsuits against him started coming out, I thought I was officially off the hook. I was actually excited to talk with you about them, because I thought it would settle things. The work was getting done. I didn't need to be the one to do it anymore.

But that's not how you saw it.

We didn't talk about my personal experience with Meat Neck again until the first lawsuit settled out of court. It barely made national news. You called me.

"You should call that lawyer. She's going to need another case," you said.

"Yeah, totally," I joked.

"I'm serious," you said.

"I'm sure she has another case lined up. If that one fails, too, maybe I'll call," I said.

Then there was a second, a third, a fourth. They all failed.

"You have to call," you said.

"I want to wait," I told you.

I didn't think anyone would listen to a sex worker if they hadn't listened to a civilian. Not only would my career be tanked, but all my future careers would be ended before they could start, too. I knew reporting him would likely end up getting me arrested.

"What he did to you is so much worse than what he did to those women," you said.

I resisted. I resisted. I resisted.

When we had been together for over two years, you told me you had a surprise for me. We didn't believe in marriage, but I still thought you might propose. You invited me to the rooftop of a college library because you read that it was the best view of Boston in the area. I got dressed up. Most of the students were away for Thanksgiving break. Before I went up to meet you, I sat for a moment watching a college kid empty library books into the return slot out of an empty beer case. I thought this was going to be a funny proposal story. But when I arrived you were in a baseball cap and there was a man on the roof with you. You were sitting at a little round table with paper cups.

"Hear him out," you said. He was young for his receding hairline, wore an ill-fitting gray suit. I pretended I knew immediately what it was all about, but I had no clue. I felt so silly.

"I heard you've had a personal encounter with Meat Neck," the man said. He did not rise. He did not reach out to shake my hand. His fingers fluttered on his coffee cup.

"You're not a lawyer," I said.

"He's a federal agent," you said.

I cinched my intercostals to keep from barfing.

"I don't care about your work," he said.

"What a relief, I totally believe you," I said.

I was embarrassed to be rude to a man in front of you because it felt not like regular rudeness but a rudeness that came out of fear. You understood that without me explaining. You put your arm around me.

"This is bigger than a lawsuit," you said.

The man nodded.

"I have nothing to say," I said.

You were quiet. You were kind. You were patient.

"Seriously, fuck you both," I said.

Leave, I told myself. But I stayed. *Cry*, I told myself because the splash of hot tears would have felt so good, but I couldn't.

"It's okay, there's no rush," the man said. He stood up. He gave me his card.

"Don't leave," you told him.

"It's okay," he said.

I kept his number for a while, just in case I thought of something to say.

But I didn't apologize to you. I just got angrier and angrier. I thought you didn't understand me. If you did, you wouldn't have put me in danger by tricking me into meeting with a government agent. If you cared about me, you would think my life was worth more than Meat Neck's failure. So, you didn't love me, I thought. I rolled that grain of sand around in my brain until it became a cyst. That cyst made me push you away. Then I acted surprised when you told me I was being mean to you, keeping you at arm's length, attacking you all the time, too sensitive to your faults.

I knew what I was doing, but I couldn't stop myself. I was young. I was hurt. I didn't yet know how to say I'm sorry, you hurt my feelings, and hear back that I had hurt yours, too. I only had enough room for one of us to be wrong, and it was you.

Turns out I was wrong twice, though. In love there is room for both people to be hurt and wrong, even about the same thing. In love this is not a sign of failure. It's embarrassingly common. But you know this. You're married now.

And I was wrong about the bigger thing, too. Meat Neck has done so much more harm than I could have imagined. If I could have prevented any of it, I should have done everything in my power to gum up the works. Maybe I couldn't have brought him down, but I could have planted the seed that later did, or maybe if I had come forward with his violence sooner, before the country was inured to him, they would have rejected him outright. Maybe. Maybe.

That's the new grain of sand. It's been growing inside me since the day I met him. Now it is bigger than me. You handed me a chance before, and I didn't take it. So this time, I had to. It seemed fitting that I'd have to pay with interest.

I hope these emails aren't a mistake. If I thought they would truly offend your sense of propriety and fidelity, I wouldn't send them. When we were breaking up, you promised not to tell anyone why, even your future partners. You said my fear of standing up for other women who were more privileged than I was—or my hesitation to do it—reflected poorly on me. You said "Objectively it looks so bad, so I won't tell anyone. I don't want you to be ostracized, but I can't be with someone with such an uncompromising perspective on identity." I said "Thank you," not because I agreed, but because I didn't want the story of my encounter with Meat Neck to get around.

I do wonder sometimes what would have happened with us if I had taken the opportunity to speak to that agent. You were wiser than I was. And you knew your way around the system. If you picked him, he probably was the right guy to turn my story into actual progress. And maybe he could have kept my identity a secret. I could have left sex work and found something else. I know you would have supported me through that. Would we still be together? If I had made the braver choice?

These letters are a time machine for you, the way this opportunity was a time machine for me. Give this letter to your younger self. I know she's still in there. She can't cheat on her partner, because she's still with me. I am her partner.

Read these and come back. Come back to the rooftop, and I'll make the other choice. I'll walk away with you, and it won't be like you're leaving your wife, because it will be like we've been together this whole time.

From: Me

To: X

October 19 at 1:59PM

Dear X,

The plan grew tighter, but the sex tape at its center never coalesced. Even I, a seasoned professional in the field of perversion, could not think of something that Meat Neck's followers would universally ditch him for. DC worried, too.

"We're not making very much progress," he said.

"This is basically a Meat Neck Sex Tape Planning Club," I said.

That was where we had stalled out when someone shot at Meat Neck. In the aftermath, the guys got morose. We saw how Meat Neck's supporters responded to his survival and everyone finally admitted that a sex tape would never work. We took the day off.

I went to Spy Pond to watch TV on my phone. I don't know what the guys did. Video games? 17 probably slept. It was a weird day in America. I got texts from a man I took economics with in college, an old coffee shop boss, a second cousin once removed. They were banal, but there was something noxious about the cluster. No one likes an event that gets men coming out of the woodwork just to text women their analysis.

My Stalker also turned up with a five-paragraph essay he had obviously written for a different worker. Haha, that's so smart, she had probably said. Now he wanted me to say it, too. That pissed me off. It made me never want to do sex work ever again, starting right then. Starting in the past, actually. I sent no texts regarding the failed assassination. I even refrained from sending the Curator a barfing emoji. Could we be friends now that I was no longer a sex worker?

My phone buzzed. Onions.

Come back to the house.

I was about to tell him I needed an afternoon off. I was about to ask him what was so urgent. But I didn't need to ask or wait. He messaged again.

We have to kill this
fucker ourselves.

From: Me

To: X

October 19 at 2:20PM

Dear X,

So we started again. DC and I took what we could from the first plan. The same gala, the same date with Meat Neck, but instead of recording a sex tape, we would kill him. I would kill him.

Let me pause for a second. Does this sound insane? I wondered, not then but later, why I didn't recoil at the idea of killing someone, even Meat Neck. I've never been a violent person. At first maybe it was shock, or disbelief. I didn't think it would actually happen. It was a relief to have different logistics to work on. I was tired of trying to figure out how the hell we were going to make a sex tape work. I was happy to have new challenges.

On TV people have nightmares after killing someone. The death haunts them. Even if they're the villain of the show. I was afraid that would happen. The only thing worse than what Meat Neck had already done to me would be Meat Neck showing up at the end of a haunted hallway in my dreams.

I decided I would worry about the ghosts if they ever arrived. I feel like there's a good chance Meat Neck's evil will mean the universe spares me. Maybe I'm deluding myself. I guess we'll find out soon.

"The security system is the biggest issue," DC said. My route to the room was designed to appear on as many CCTV tapes as possible, so we could use the footage to help prove the sex tape was real. "At least we have the hotel all mapped out, that's a place to start," DC said.

"What are you talking about?" Onions said.

"Security cameras on the way in," DC said.

"I think I can disable those," Walnuts said.

"You think?" I said.

"This isn't a game," DC said.

"I know I can," Walnuts said.

"It's true—he does it at the mall," Onions said.

"I don't want to know more about the mall," DC said.

"A mall is totally different than a hotel," I said.

"Is it?" DC said.

The next thing we had to figure out was the murder weapon. The guys were most enthusiastic about a gun or a bowie knife.

"A gun is too loud," I said.

"And you'll never get it in the hotel," DC said.

"What if it's already in the hotel?" Onions said.

"How?" I said.

"I don't know, plant it early? Someone else brings it in? An employee who won't get searched?" Onions said.

"They search everyone," DC said.

"Yeah, that's dumb," Walnuts said.

"Okay, sorry. It won't work, just an idea," Onions said.

A bowie knife could also not pass a search, but it wouldn't be as loud and could be easier to plant in advance. Still, it seemed risky. If someone did see it, there's no way it could pass as anything innocent. 17 wanted me to strangle Meat Neck. He was a real garrote freak. (I don't meet too many new kinds of freaks these days. I've met dudes who are into strangulation, but 17 is the only garrote freak I've ever met.) I let Onions, Eyebrows, and Walnuts fight. I said no to 17. We all said no to 17.

"My girl hands aren't strong enough," I joked.

"No, you don't get the physics. You use a bar of some kind to—" 17 said.

"Okay," said Onions, "not—no, just not that."

DC thought we should use poison. The murder would be untraceable and the poison would give us time to clear the area. I agreed that was wise, but I didn't like the idea because I knew the real reason they were saying I should use poison was because they thought I wasn't capable of anything else. You know me. Nothing makes me more stubborn than being underestimated. I didn't have a better idea, though.

"How will we get the poison in?" DC asked.

"We could put it into a tiny container? Like disposable eye drops?" I said.

We both liked this. It would be easier to pour a tiny container into a drink than draw a syringe in the heat of the moment. We started collecting little vials to test out. Even resealable eyedrops proved too leaky. A travel bottle of makeup remover might work, but it would be way bigger than we needed. It was 17 who thought of the perfume sample.

I started crashing at the house in Somerville. I justified it with late planning sessions, but really, I was watching my old life scab over, and I didn't want to disturb the universe's progress toward erasing me. I gave up my lease, got rid of all my stuff. A new woman moved into my apartment. At night, I planned my exit from the country.

I figured if anyone came looking for me they would assume I was just a sex worker who had gone missing or run away.

I thought I would miss that apartment. I thought it meant a lot to me because it was my first place of my own. But it turns out my attachment to it wasn't that deep. Hell, this house practically feels like it's mine after a single night of squatting. I say that as I contemplate how good, but also dumb, it would be to start up the wood-fired Japanese soaking tub.

God, I wish you were here. It's a shame I can't fully enjoy the place. What I wouldn't give for an hour to scrub my body half-raw and sit in the cedar bath. Use the fluffy towels. Make a fire. Lay on the imported tile floor of the solarium and read. Instead, I try to memorize the sandalwood smell of the closets, the particular blue-gray of the bedroom walls, the sisal rug and the wool rug and the turquoise silk rug. There is an oil painting of a Shaker bonnet that makes me feel warm and afraid and I wonder who the artist is and why I can't stop staring at it. There's no real reason to memorize it. I just want to enjoy it all and I don't have the time to do that properly now.

Material things don't matter. In the last ten years I have forgotten that a little, but it's only because things have kept me better company than people. I dated after you, a lot in the beginning and less as time went on. At first I thought my desire for what we had had was juvenile, then deluded, then that maybe I was misremembering. Then I thought maybe we all just get older and less capable of ardor. But you were ten years older than me. It wasn't about age. It was about us.

Understand why I'm telling you all this. It's a vain desire. "Without someone to recognize you, do you even exist?" you asked me once, at the height of our love.

Well, here it is, the full story, selfishly, my whole and deepest truth. Look. Before I fully disappear, I imagine myself existing for one second: cohesive, shiny, at my best, for your eyes only.

I promise. I'm almost done.

September drew to an end. Our time was running out.

From: Me

To: X

October 19 at 3:06PM

Dear X,

I had a hospital pharmacist connection in Back Bay who could help with the poison. He was a retired sex worker himself who liked to keep in touch with people still in the trade. It made him feel comparatively accomplished.

"There's nothing fun about this shit," he told me when I told him what I was looking for.

"It's an audition," I explained. "I have a client who has a frenemy who wants to stock it."

The frenemy said it was impossible to get. The client wanted to prove a point. He came to me. It sounded like something a stupid client would do.

"Okay," the pharmacist said.

I asked DC to pick it up with me.

We had become something like friends. Work friends. I liked being around him and he clearly felt the same. There had even been moments in the work so far when I felt preemptively sad about how I would have to say goodbye to him at the end of the job. Maybe I would have felt differently if he ever talked about his politics, but he didn't mention them, so it was easy for me to imagine he wasn't a white supremacist. I mean, I was there, and I wasn't a white supremacist, either.

We went to get the drugs on a Saturday morning. The exchange was quick. My friend was wearing his lab coat, because he was allegedly on his way to work. We agreed to hang out soon. I handed him more money than he made in a month, because I liked to remind the people who'd gotten out of the trade that they should watch the condescension.

When I got back to the car, DC had moved to the passenger seat.

"I'm relieved we're actually making some progress. I should have taken over this operation from the start," I said. He laughed.

"Yes, you really sat back and let everyone flounder instead of secretly fixing things behind the scenes," he said.

As morbid as it sounds, I was having fun.

My phone rang.

"Spoke too soon?" DC said.

"Hello?" I said.

"Are you alone?" Walnuts' voice quavered.

"Yes?" I said.

"I need your help," he said.

"What?" I said.

"I can't get to Meat Neck. I know I said I could. I should have told you earlier. I don't know what to do," he said.

I hadn't seen this coming, but I wasn't at all surprised. I suppressed a chuckle.

"No problem," I said. I didn't have an immediate solution, but I was pretty confident I could figure it out.

"I posted like sixty ads and I thought it would work but he didn't respond to any of them," he said.

"You did what?"

"It seemed like it would work—" he started.

"I will handle it." I hung up.

I was energized, which thank God. My brain whirred into action. I texted the Curator.

At your office? I said. Immediate thumbs-up.

OMW, I wrote.

"We have to make another stop," I told DC.

The Curator was having a smoke outside the bookstore she called her office. She is a petite blond woman with big green eyes, a round nose, thin lips, and the vestiges of a Nashville accent. She was wearing pressed linen shorts and thin gold strands around her wrists and neck that looked more like 24k gold-plated weapons than delicate jewelry. She had an amethyst

Birkin that, if it was a fake, was a superfake. I don't like blondes, but she is irresistible. DC ogled her.

"You stay here," I told DC. The Curator looked at DC and I saw her eyes widen for just a second before she quickly looked away. Did she recognize him from something?

"I'm so happy to see you," she said. She touched my forearms. How long had it been since I'd gotten laid? I forgot about DC for a second.

"I am looking for an intro to Meat Neck," I said.

"Girl, yes," she said. It was enthusiasm, not an answer, but it was a good start. "Let's go for a walk," she said.

"We'll be right back," I yelled through the glass.

"You took the keys!" he yelled back. He looked ill.

What was wrong with him? The Curator had her back turned for all of this in a borderline pointed way. I wondered if she had her own experience with DC somehow. She worked with some pretty nasty people. Maybe she was in with the neo-Nazi crowd. I guessed it would make sense that she wouldn't want to acknowledge him. But she acknowledged way worse people. He wasn't a high roller. Maybe she was embarrassed because he wasn't a high roller?

I couldn't help myself.

"Do you know him?" I asked.

"Oh, hmm, yeah," she said.

We were walking at a clip now, toward the end of a long shady block.

"Where do you know him from?" she said.

"Work," I said.

"Me too," she said.

Her intonation was confusing, but I didn't really want to get into it, because I didn't want to talk about men with her, and if I did, I only wanted it to be for work. For necessary work. So I was glad when we turned the corner and she changed the topic.

"Have you been traveling? Go anywhere nice?" she said.

"No, you?"

"Miami, Morocco. I'm going to Japan in a few weeks," she said.

"I've never been."

She grabbed my arm.

"You *have* to go. I don't want to spoil it. I'll just say: baboons."

Baboons? What the fuck did that mean?

Talking to the Curator is like talking to a fairy-tale witch. The longer you talk, the longer you want to stay. The longer you stay, the more she extracts down the line. She was an absolute magician when it came to getting you to promise things you wanted to promise, then making you pay with whatever it stung to lose. And like a witch, she was my last chance. Thank God I was planning to disappear. Would the disappearance I had planned be enough, though? If the Curator wanted to find me, it was likely she could. More likely than neo-Nazis or federal agents. Fuck.

The blocks in that part of the city were long, full of red town houses and old trees. The Curator kept to the shade. Little spots of sun periodically freckling her face.

"So what's up, girly?" she said.

"Oh, it's kind of awkward—" I started. But she cut me off.

"What happened to that girl you matched with? The one with the white leather coat."

I chuckled.

"Oh yeah, it worked out, we're married now, got a white leather couch." She giggled.

I felt something hulking behind us. A car? But no one was there.

"What about you? Are you dating?" I asked.

"Same guy back home," she said.

"The carpenter," I said.

"Woodworker," she said.

The Curator's life (or cover story) was a Hallmark Christmas movie, and I was glad I'd never get to the bottom of which.

"Oh, but I'm adopting a Cavapoo!" she said.

We stopped to look at photos of the puppy. We U-turned.

I tried to cover as much distance back to the shop as I could before bringing up the favor again. Maybe this was her way of telling me I shouldn't have asked in the first place, but that she liked me, so she was giving me an out? If I read the room and didn't ask again, I'd be home free. But it was too late for that. I had to ask. We entered the gate in front of the bookstore. DC was slumped in the front passenger seat with his eyes closed and his legs dangling out the door.

She turned so her back was to the car.

"So how *do* you know DC?" she said.

"How do you know DC?" I said.

"Same way you do?" she said. Her tone was mysterious, though.

"Same way I do?" I said.

"Why do you need to get to Meat Neck?"

"What?"

"No, sorry, you don't need to tell me. I know you're not a fan. If he were already your client, you'd have his number. Unless he's blocked you. Did he block you?" she said.

"No," I said.

"Exactly."

She nodded toward DC.

"So how do you know him?" she said.

"Work," I said.

"He's a fed, so what does that make you? I know you're not an undercover agent . . . Confidential informant?" she said. My face went white. I wanted to hurl.

It all began to click: how we had been able to get Meat Neck's schedule, how we were able to get Meat Neck's security detail information, the hotel security rundown. A fed. He had been quietly pulling strings this whole time.

"Are *you* a confidential informant?" I said.

"Oh, no, or from time to time, I guess. I don't know. I don't know him that well. What's he like? He's such a mystery," she said.

"He's nice? And efficient?" I said. "He has a corny sense of humor."

"Totally," she said. "Well, tell him I say hi?"

"You just said hi," I said.

“Oh, right.”

“Okay, I have to go?” I said.

“So, Meat Neck. I’ll send you a number, just text it,” she said.

“Oh, thank you?”

“No problem! What’s mine is yours!”

She blew DC a kiss. I got back in the driver’s seat.

“You’re a fucking federal agent?” I said.

From: Me

To: X

October 19 at 3:55PM

Dear X,

"Fuck, she told you. I'm so sorry," he said.

"Explain," I said.

To his credit, he was sweating. His face looked like wet clay. A federal agent in the mix meant what? I tried to spur my brain to conclusions, but it wasn't working. I turned up the AC.

"I like you. When all this started, before you joined, I didn't realize they'd implicate—?" he said.

"Implicate what?" I said.

"A non-Nazi?" he said. I shook my head.

My guts, which had, before this afternoon, been normal guts, organs you can ignore almost every day of the year, had hardened into squirming, acidic ropes. I kind of wanted to die. At least, I wanted to be somewhere very far from my body.

"Go back. You're, what? Surveilling these white supremacists, so someone can build a case against them and put them in jail?"

He looked at me like I was stupid.

"There's not exactly a budget for taking down small-scale neo-Nazi wannabes," he said. It *had* felt like he wasn't one of us. Coalition building, I reminded myself. But at what cost?! A federal agent with a front row seat to the whole plot?

"Well, if you're not here to take us down—" I said.

DC stared at me blankly. It came to me.

"You're here to make sure we succeed?" I said.

He said nothing.

"Then what? I'm arrested, I guess. But I'm not even a Nazi!" I said.

"Well, you will be a murderer, though," he said.

"Because you planned this whole thing!" I said. "So I'm fucked."

"I'm so sorry," he said. Why wasn't he correcting me? Why wasn't he reassuring me?

"Am I fucked?"

He shrugged.

We drove home in silence. I wasn't even angry. I had no feelings at all. My body was just hot and shaking. When we got to the house, I went up to my room. I didn't know what else to do. What would you do, X?

I felt like absolute shit. When we got back, the kitchen smelled like a prom. 17 had rinsed half a dozen tiny perfume samples and left them to dry on the tines of the drying rack.

I had completely screwed myself. I had ruined my life.

Then I realized I was catastrophizing and that my self-blame was not a step in the right direction but a diversion. I needed to take a break.

From: Me

To: X

October 19 at 4:15PM

Dear X,

I needed to think. I got in the shower.

I had less than two weeks to fix things, and until I knew what that was going to entail, there wasn't time to rest. I wondered if it was the whole government that wanted Meat Neck dead or if DC represented some rogue actors. You had already proved to me that there were people in our own government who thought Meat Neck was a threat when you found a federal agent willing to meet with me all those years ago. DC could be the natural conclusion of that.

But I didn't have time for the why; I had to figure out what I was going to do, and how. I was not going down with this ship.

My first thought was that I should quit. I could run away, I figured, with the money I had put aside. If I left now, maybe no one would even come after me.

Yes, that's what I would do. I rinsed my hair. I threw on clothes. Honestly, I considered calling you. But no, I couldn't call anyone. Should I take everything with me? If the house was being watched, someone would notice that. I got dressed. I filled my gym bag with cash and my purse with a change of clothes.

The guys weren't home to watch me leave. I walked to the end of the block, then I walked all the way to the T station. If anyone was following me, I didn't spot them.

I took the T to Central Square, got out, went into a bookstore. But standing there, looking at the wall of flyers advertising nannies and guitar lessons and local chiropractic care, I still felt numb. I wandered around looking at books for a minute. I watched a young bookseller wearing a bolo tie and a pin that said "BISEXUAL EMPIRE" walk into the biography aisle, pick up the Meat Neck bio, and tuck it back behind the rest of the books. It was a tiny act. It would be undone by the next bookseller who passed, probably. It was already a bestseller.

They caught me catching them and chuckled.

That's when I realized that what had begun as bluster at that first meeting in the bar was now muscle. I had learned to do the work by doing it.

I didn't need to know what *you* would do to fix this, X, but what would *I* do? So far, the job had required so many different skills. This was the next test. I didn't need connections or research or flirtation or geometry or geography or current events or even charm. I needed to win DC to my side. And there was only one surefire way I could think to do that.

I took DC for a walk that evening.

"Are we being followed?" I asked.

"Nah, too dangerous with this level of cover," he said.

"What if I run before we do it?"

"The people I work for would come get you. Intent to commit the crime is also a crime."

"Which people you work for?"

He rolled his eyes, which I knew meant he wasn't talking about the ones who couldn't plan their own sex tape.

"That's what I thought."

Unrelatedly, I had a really bad blister on the back of my heel, and I wanted to stop walking, but I didn't really believe we weren't being followed and moving felt safer.

"You must think I'm evil, to be doing this. What kind of person would get mixed up with a bunch of Nazis trying to kill a guy? Or maybe you just think sex workers have bad morals," I said.

"You know I don't think that," he said. DC believed he was more open-minded than most men, like every other man.

I took a deep breath. I knew what I had to do but I wasn't quite ready. DC took my silence and ran with it.

"Don't feel bad. Really. It's all about access to resources and inequality. You're a caring person. I can see that. If things were different, I think you'd be a really natural mother."

Shit was getting weird. Mother?

"Are you calling me nurturing?"

"I should have said strong. You're really strong. Most men couldn't do half the things you've done in your life."

What things, I wanted to say. Instead, I skipped that part. I had to tell him.

"Look, this is personal for me. Meat Neck—one of the people Meat Neck—one of his victims is someone close to me." I looked down and focused on making my eyes water.

"Oh God," he said. He stopped. We were across the street from a small park overrun with kids. An ice cream truck passed. I felt sad, which I had not expected.

"Do you need to sit down?" he asked.

But we started walking again instead.

After letting one tear run slowly down my face, I told him it was me, not someone close to me. I tried to think of what to say next. Then I stopped trying. I didn't share many details. We walked over an hour, crossing through half a dozen different neighborhoods. I listened to people talking in English, Korean, Arabic, and finally Portuguese. I listened to car tires, and horns, and radios. I listened to DC tell me about the mandatory sexual assault training course they had to take when working for the government, and how some of the stories had really affected him. We heard balls bouncing off walls and smelled barbecue, but didn't know from where. Finally, we stopped in front of a redbrick Catholic church with white trim.

"So what can I do?" he said.

Bingo.

"I mean, I'm so sorry, this is so fucked-up. If something like that happened to my sister?" he said. He didn't finish the sentence, though.

I had this strange thought then, that if he was undercover it meant he wasn't actually a Nazi, and I hadn't really put that together yet. I had thought of his identities as stacked on one another instead of as foils or lies.

"Help me," I said, without thinking. I didn't mean to shiver, but I did. I didn't realize the fear had already found its way into my body until then.

"I'm scared of being arrested, or killed," I said. I cried a little. I didn't have to try. It turned out I was scared.

"Okay," he said. He touched my arm. I could tell he didn't like to see me shiver. As much as I hated my own unintentional display of weakness, I wonder now if it was the thing that made the difference.

"Let me live free," I said. I spoke slowly, so my voice would be clear and strong.

"Okay," he said.

"Okay?"

"Well, I'm really going to try," he said. He squeezed my arm and pulled his mouth into that worried kind of frown that's meant to reassure you.

I shouldn't complain. I'm not complaining. But it never ceases to amaze me how quickly a guy gets upset about a woman he knows.

We returned to the house. The next day, work started again, as usual. I texted the number the Curator sent me, chatted with a man who asked for my ID. I sent him the same fake I usually use for jobs and held my breath as he checked me out.

Meanwhile we kept working on other things. The guys were a little more certain than I was that Meat Neck's team would care about the public knowing he'd spent his final hours with an escort. But I was more worried that Meat Neck would recognize me and cancel the date, or that the police would want to question the sex worker he'd been with right before he dropped dead of a heart attack. I gave the guy my availability for his New York dates and my rate, and he confirmed the night of the gala.

Need tix? he said.

Nope, already got 'em, I said.

Nice!

He dropped a sizable tip in my account.

DC told me he had found a way to keep the area around Meat Neck's hotel room clear for almost a full hour. If I could act quickly, I would have time to leave before his own government team arrived to take over and arrest me. He seemed sure it would work. I wasn't so sure. Things were way too murky for my taste.

What would you have done? You probably wouldn't have wound up in this situation in the first place. Did I think it was the strongest plan? No. Did I fully trust DC at this point? Also no. But I was pretty sure moving forward was the only option I had that could still work out in my favor. Basically, I was relying on the same logic Wile E. Coyote uses when confronted with a cliff.

The job had always been real, but this was when it started to feel like it was going to actually happen. That is, my body felt like it was a living countdown clock, ticking toward the moment I would be in the same room as Meat Neck again. At first it felt like little pinpricks of anger effervescing through me at the slightest provocation. In a way that felt good, like rubbing alcohol on a bug bite. I would think about it on purpose sometimes. But when the thoughts started happening on their own, they began to feel less exciting and more stressful. I'd be walking and feel a hardness in my gut that almost knocked the wind out of me. Or I would have a nightmare I couldn't remember, but that somehow still left Meat Neck's face emblazoned on the backs of my eyelids. I reminded myself that seeing him in person would be different this time. I was older now. I was sure of myself. I had a mission.

From: Me

To: X

October 19 at 4:40PM

Dear X,

On October 17 we all separately found our way to New York. We convened in an empty apartment that belonged to Onions' friend. Walnuts had everything labeled and organized, laid out on the kitchen counter. We stood in a U around it. I drank my coffee and felt very professional, competent, chill.

"Where are the gala tickets?" DC asked.

"Go into your photos app?" Walnuts said.

"On my phone?" DC said.

Walnuts huffed. DC held out his phone. Walnuts took it.

"Here," he said.

"This is just a screenshot," DC said.

"Yeah, how do you think tickets work? When was the last concert you went to? Have you gotten on a plane lately?" Walnuts said.

DC did seem like a bit of a Luddite. But I, too, was surprised. We opened the tickets. They looked like tickets.

"How hard was this to make?" DC said.

"Why?" said Walnuts.

"Just, you really bragged about being able to make these. What is this, Photoshop?"

"Are you fucking serious, man? Do you know how hard it is to perfectly mimic something that looks this simple?"

"What time is it?" I asked. "I'm going to change."

But no one responded, so I didn't move right away. I didn't want to miss anything.

"I'm heading out," Onions said. He collected his gear: a single-use packet of superglue, two syringes, two needles, and the drugs all folded together in a pouch.

Eyebrows took a little black pen that was apparently pepper spray, though it was unclear who it was supposed to be for. We all had earbuds that connected us to Walnuts.

In the bathroom, time felt briefly limitless. I slid on my tights and pulled up my hair to do my makeup. I remember when you and I were together and putting on makeup still felt like putting on a costume. Now it feels like putting on a shirt. It's not part of my body, but I would never go out without it. It's a persona. A persona that protects the real me. I primed my face. I applied color corrector. Usually, it's the smell of the color corrector that numbs my brain, calls forward the softer, dumber form of myself, the version of me that can walk and talk and fuck and entertain without my full brain. But it took longer this time. I put on concealer. I started my eyes.

When I finished, I looked amazing, but I felt more like myself than I was used to. Was it because I had taken a break from sex work?

Someone knocked on the door. I jumped.

"You ready?" It was Walnuts.

I pulled up the sleeves of my dress and let down my hair. There was no more time to try to get into character. This was going to have to be the character.

Walnuts went up to "the control center" via the lobby. DC and I met behind the building, because we needed a minute before heading in, and it's hard to find a good place to stand in New York City. Or maybe it's easy to find a good place. Maybe any place is a good place to stand in New York City and we were just from Boston.

It felt oddly appropriate to be standing on the loading dock of a hotel in formal wear. I wore a black silk gown with a T-back and a deep V neckline that stopped right above my belly button. I also wore flat pointed leather boots, because Meat Neck hated for women to be able to look him in the eye.

"Are you sure no one's going to see us?" I asked.

"Walnuts deactivated the exterior cameras," DC said.

We both clocked the same camera, right above the exterior door, red light on. *Maybe red light means the camera is off?*

"I'm starting to doubt that guy," DC said.

"Mics are hot," Walnuts said.

An onset of beeping heralded the backward arrival of a truck, and we hopped off the ledge and jogged out of the way. The gala had started. The exterior fundraiser decor was half-assed, but it was an ornate half-assing at least: a temporary golden water feature, lights, and flowers, but no one had asked the halal cart out front to move and a family in I ♥ NY T-shirts was pushing through the revolving door into the hotel. There were half a dozen security guards with coil-tubed earpieces and muscles so large they looked like cartoons. It reminded me of this client I used to have who was obsessed with pointing out which men's muscles came from the gym, and which came from "honest work." He had the honest work muscles, but he had attained them by being really specific at the gym, he said.

I approached the revolving door.

"Miss," said a cartoon strongman, "are you here for the event?"

See, I projected silently over my shoulder toward DC, while also attempting to project an aura that I was alone, *they're just going to let me in—you just have to know what you're doing and go with confidence.*

"Yes," I said.

"I need to see your ticket," he said.

"Oh, I spaced," I said. Up close there were minor variations between the strongmen. They were all different ages, but they had the same hairstyle, the same stretched and pore-less ochre-tinted faces. DC stepped forward.

"I have them both," he said.

Strongman tilted his head to see the ticket. He frowned. He opened his phone and scanned it.

A cheerful little noise gwonked.

"Sir, all right if I hold your phone for a moment?" Strongman said.

"Sure?" said DC.

Strongman scanned again. Gwonk. He handed the phone back. He stepped into a circle of Strongmens. They nodded and frowned.

"This isn't good," DC said.

"At least the cameras are all deactivated," I said. Wherever I looked under the hotel awning, little red lights winked at me.

Inside the hotel lobby I could see people in evening wear posing in front of a violet-and-yellow step-and-repeat emblazoned with the right wing's favorite snack food and national defense brands.

"Did you buy these tickets?" Strongman asked.

I jumped. I hadn't seen him return. He was a very agile guy.

"Yes?" DC said.

We were going to have to have a talk about all this upspeak, I decided.

"That's what I thought. Someone sold counterfeit tickets, I'm afraid," he said.

"Uh-oh," said Walnuts in our ears.

"What?" DC said. He looked like he was about to cry.

"That's outrageous! We paid a lot of money for these," I said.

"I'm really sorry," Strongman said.

I waited for DC to say something, to solve it. Nothing.

"Can we buy new tickets now?" I asked.

"I'm afraid not, strict policy," he said.

"Surely there must be room for a few extra people," I said. The funny thing was, as soon as our tickets hadn't worked, my trepidation over being recognized by Meat Neck was eclipsed by a desperate need for our plan to work.

"Ha, yeah. Thing is, they don't want anyone in there who wasn't previously vetted. You have to pass a background check to get in or be a guest of a VIP. There's been too many recent, uh—incidents," he said.

"Wait, why don't they run background checks on guests of VIPs?" DC asked.

Strongman looked confused. Strongman looked sad that DC was such a dummy. Strongman looked apologetic that I was with such a dummy.

"He means the girlfriends," I said.

"Girlfriends." Strongman nodded.

"Girlfriends aren't going to shoot up the place," I said.

Another couple approached. Nice big age gap on those two. I kicked myself for not taking the ticket Meat Neck's guy had offered.

"Let's get out of the way. Hey, next time, how can we be sure we're not getting fake tickets?" I said.

"Oh, well, just read the offer really well. If anything is misspelled or if the email address looks crazy, then it's probably a scam," he said.

"Oh, wow, genius, thank you," I said.

DC was pulling me away.

"Walnuts, did you actually scalp these tickets instead of make them?" I said.

"Maybe," Walnuts said.

"I'm going to make a call," DC said. He popped out his earbud and handed it to me. I watched him type out a text message. Then I watched him wait for a response.

If I let my mind wander, nervousness began to wash in. I wouldn't be able to do my job if it set up shop, so I needed to do something to stop it. As if on cue, DC gave me a problem to solve.

"We have to find some other place to stand. We stick out here," he said.

"We just look like we're taking a smoke break," I said.

There was a cluster of tuxedos actually taking a smoke break twenty feet down the block. DC's phone rang.

"Why can't we just rent a room, like Walnuts?" I said.

"Won't work. Walnuts checked in a week ago, before they started prepping for the gala. Anyone checking in today got prescreened as well. I could probably get in but—" He stopped.

So it was because of me. He could have gotten through because he worked for the government. A background check on me would have inspired more investigation than he felt we could risk. That's to say nothing of the times I had gotten arrested at protests.

"I could go in as a girlfriend?" I said.

"Can I get a little privacy?" DC said.

Now he was huffy. I threw my hands up and walked toward the smokers. I wasn't relying on anyone but myself to get this job done.

"Can I get a cigarette? Or—are you vaping?" I asked.

It took me a second to process who I had asked. They were famous men. They looked just as surprised as I was that I had casually spoken to them. You know someone's political support has gone mainstream when outside a public fundraiser, surrounded by photographers, you find a Gen Xer with a superhero franchise, transition lenses, and the murk of bisexuality chatting it up with more than one pallid but jacked, bug-eyed sex symbol with line cook energy.

One of the line cooks gave me a rollie, and I swear it's been worth every word in these emails just to get to tell you that. It was stupidly cliché. A line cook? A rollie? This particular line cook had been a child star.

The men were talking about producer credits.

I was a little starstruck by the tuxedos. One of the men was someone I'd spent a lot of energy recently trying to figure out if he was hot-hot or just hot because he was famous.

"So, what's up, you all in a biopic about how Meat Neck becomes the next Hitler?"

The Superhero grinned. Then they all did.

"You're funny," said Child Star.

"Just like Eva Braun," I said.

"Really?" said the younger line cook.

"No, idiot, Eva Braun wasn't funny," said Child Star. I liked him better. I had always liked him better. I wondered if the fact that he was my favorite line-cook-coded actor would mean he would bring me inside.

"You're funny," I said.

"Funny's just a nasty word for not-handsome," said Child Star.

"So what am I?" I said.

He inhaled deeply. Whatever he was sucking on had some weed in it.

"Here? You're a plain Jane if I ever saw one," Child Star huffed.

I laughed hard.

"And you're a piece of shit," I said.

"At least I know it," he said. He was smiling. He was smiling like he knew I was too good for him, which was a charming trick.

"You need a date to this thing?" I said. I was feeling good. My persona had clocked in. She was late, but I loved her.

He smirked.

"Nope," he said.

"That's too bad, because I do," I said.

He chuckled.

"Okay, you can't take me in, but can you do me a favor—can you introduce me to that guy over there?" I pointed at a potential smoker who seemed to be on a fake phone call near the real smokers.

"I don't know that guy. Why that guy?" he asked.

"Does it matter? It will work."

"Okay, I'm curious," he said.

"But if this works, you can't rat me out," I said.

He literally crossed his heart.

We walked toward the man. He noticed we were coming and recoiled, then tried not to spring forward in his enthusiasm.

"Excuse me, this is my friend. She wants to meet you, but she's too shy," Child Star said.

The man was confused. The man was transfixed. The man stuck out his hand to shake my hand.

"Nice to meet you," he said. He wasn't looking at me, he was looking at Child Star.

"I'll meet you inside?" I said.

Child Star gave me a salute.

"Uh, shouldn't we go with him?" the man said.

"In a minute. Let's just chat for a second. I'm tired of the air-conditioning," I said.

The same guard who didn't let me in before gave me a wink and a thumbs-up this time. I like to think he was proud of me. I like to think he was proud of us for having a successful subtextual conversation where he told me how to get in and I heard him and achieved it. It's possible he'd just already forgotten me or really believed that "girlfriends" were safe. Underestimating women is almost too easy to accuse these assholes of out loud. Yet here we are. I wish I were making this up.

The lobby smelled like white musk, sandalwood, and cognac. It was actually very nice. Maybe these fundraisers are trashy in other places, but once you got past the decorations outside, this one in New York lived up to the city. It was like going to the opera on a night where everyone dresses up. I caught a man staring at me from the bar and thought maybe he was an undercover agent there to help DC, but when I got a little closer, I saw it was just a man I had worked with before. He turned to the bartender with an oily grin that could only have been meant to deflect my attention.

"No shit, you don't actually want to hear about being a child star—it doesn't matter," Child Star was saying as we walked up. There were babes around him now, but he was talking to a man. He had such precise elocution.

The man who'd walked me in had dentures as bright as a grill. He pushed a wineglass at me.

"No, thank you," I said.

"You a fan?" Dentures said.

I shrugged toward Child Star.

"Just friends," I said.

"Not him, Meat Neck," he said. "Why would I care about him?"

"Hey!" Child Star said.

"Why would I be here if I weren't a Meat Neck fan?" I said.

"Why indeed," Dentures said. He took his wine back and walked away.

"I'm going to the bar," I said.

I stepped into a vestibule to text the number the Curator had given me.

Confirming for tonight, I said. I sent a selfie with his security team in the background.

Someone replied with a bouquet emoji.

I heard my name again and jumped. My persona fled the scene. I kicked myself for taking three months off sex work. All my calibrations were off. I was too sensitive in places I should be numb, I was vigilant where I should ignore danger, I was probably missing actual signs of danger. I turned around.

It was DC.

"How did you get in?" I asked.

"How did *you* get in?" he asked.

"I'm a professional," I said.

"Me too," he said.

Banter. The banter helped. Conversation helped. Things I knew how to do made me feel better. "We're good to go," I said. I tapped my purse, where the poison was hidden.

A Strongman appeared with an envelope for me. Cash. Cash helped.

"You can go up anytime," he said.

"Anytime?" I said.

"He has a full bar up there. His guy can let you in," he said.

DC waited for Strongman to walk away. Then he waited a beat longer. He leaned in to whisper.

"You have to stay with the body after he's dead. You have to wait long enough that he can't be resuscitated. An hour at least, to be absolutely certain. Two is preferable, so the team can clear the area. The longer you wait, the more it will look like a heart attack, because the fewer people he will have been in contact with who would have noticed something," DC said.

I nodded.

"Don't acknowledge," he said.

I started to nod again, but caught myself.

He was building himself a little cover. The guys would be able to hear him, but so would whoever he actually worked for. His boss would know he had told me to stay put.

The real plan was for me to leave as soon as Meat Neck was down and the hallway was clear. This would give me time to escape and DC plausible deniability when I failed to turn up at our meeting point, then he showed up at the room and found only the corpse. Although for this to work, he had to not freak out and he was looking pretty gray again.

"You can't just wait outside for me. I need privacy," I said.

This was as close as I could come to reminding him of our deal.

He nodded. "You ready for this?"

I was surprised to find that my persona was still gone, but my heart was strong and slow.

"Yes."

"I know you are," he said.

I spotted a camera in the elevator going up to Meat Neck's floor. I kept my face down, but there wasn't anything else I could think to do. Assuming everything went right, soon everyone would know about his death, and in order to get through this I had to believe that Walnuts had actually deactivated the cameras.

I did not believe for one second he had deactivated them.

I arrived at the right door and knocked. Meat Neck's man walked out. I walked in.

From: Me
To: X
October 19 at 5:20PM

Dear X,

I'm almost to the end. It's late afternoon/early evening now. I do wish you were here. You used to give the best back massages. My whole body is rigid from exertion and anxiety.

Is some small part of you jealous that it was me who got this opportunity instead of you? I think of your rage and how much you like to expend it. I think of your efficiency. But this couldn't have been you. It could only be me. It was me who was suited for it. It was me who grew into the role, whenever growth was needed. It was me who found fatal flaws in the plan and made changes. I can't believe it took me quite this long to see that I'm not just as good as you, but better.

Does it come as a surprise to hear me talk this way? This is me now. Don't you like it? How many nights have you appeared in my dreams, and I've woken up with a sore throat, hollow and sad. I have settled for photos of you online, rereading old emails, imagining your side of hypothetical conversations. I know I'm remembering you better than you were. That's common enough. We all do that. I'm sure you do the same with me. Only now you know: I am better than I was, I'm even better than you remember.

I've decided to leave the country as soon as I finish this. I guess I'll probably never come back unless I get a pardon. Another thing this adventure has done is polished off any extant death wish.

I am sure you can figure out where I'm going. It's exactly the place you think it is, because it's the place you said you wanted to go. Thanks for that idea, by the way. Just another piece of this that I might have considered a debt, if I hadn't recently recognized that you don't owe someone for having an idea you use, if you use it better than they ever will.

I do have one favor to ask you. You don't owe me, either, but I hope you will do it as a gift to me. I need a grace period before you share these emails or even the fact of their existence with your wife. That's the one risk I'm not prepared to take. You can imagine why I'm not prepared to trust her with a story this juicy. She's got no reason to protect me. But I'm so in love with you, so sure about us, that I weighed the likelihood of you ignoring this request and still started typing. Now you can surely understand the other reason I hit send on the first email wasn't just in case of my imminent death but also so that I wouldn't lose my nerve before I got to the end. This is my last vulnerable gift to you.

Just one more thing before I finish, which I hope you can forgive, if you don't accept: You should consider joining me. This is the real thing—you know it. You just have to decide if you're brave enough for it. This was my one crazy chance to get you back, and I took it. I'm not going to be coy and say maybe you have something better than what we had. I know you don't. You may have an amalgamation of things more important, or a constellation of things you can't leave. Or you may have changed. You may have sold out. I'm joking, but I'm not joking.

I don't know exactly how long you will have to wait. I can't imagine it will take that long, maybe a month, a few, a year at most. You'll know when the time is right.

Now to finish. Sorry in advance. It's gruesome. I think you'll like it.

I tried to stick to the plan, despite being rattled. The plan was to go in, get a lay of the land, wait for Meat Neck to arrive, establish rapport, ask for a drink, pour poison in his. But Meat Neck was already in the room when I got there. He must have come up just ahead of me, while his guy was giving me the envelope. He was older than he looked online, and exponentially older than when I'd last seen him. His eyes were ringed in greenish-yellow circles. He smelled like nothing—not even skin, not even air.

"It *is* you," he said.

I felt simultaneously numb and like every part of my body was screaming with pain.

"Me," I said.

He quirked his head to the side. His mouth slid upward at the ends. On other faces it would have been considered a smile. He had recognized me. Did he know where he knew me from? Either he just didn't give a fuck or this was another layer of his sick games.

"I'll take this," he said. Before I had a chance to process what he was doing, he took my purse.

He made drinks. I went to the bathroom. I opened a drawer to look for something with a rope to strangle him with. Nothing. I opened a black leather dopp kit and found a switchblade in with his toiletries. There was toothpaste residue on the handle. I scratched it off and I put the knife in my boot.

I used the toilet. I went back out. I tried to get to my purse. I was glad for 17's dumb sleight-of-hand training. Though I didn't get a chance to use it to get my purse back. I was extremely aware of the time. The longer the assassination took, the less time I had to escape. We had words. Meat Neck was jolly. We moved to the bed. Meat Neck got on top of me. Then Meat Neck wanted me to get on top of him. We were still fully clothed.

Then Meat Neck said before we "do this" he was going to order some room service and did I like potato skins, and I thought, *Fuck, time's up*, and I stabbed him as hard as I could in what Walnuts had promised was the liver.

Meat Neck didn't have a chance to look scared. He did look a little angry. My fist was up against his skin and I pushed the knife deeper and upward, hoping to cut as much as possible, hoping to speed up the bleeding. He shook a few times. I couldn't tell why at first. Then I realized he was coughing. Then his chest hissed and I thought maybe I'd hit a lung? There was blood coming out of his mouth. There was no way to make any of it look like an accident now.

I went to wash my hands in the bathroom and when I came back, his eyes were open, but he was very dead.

For one second, everything was good.

Then the phone rang.

The phone was not supposed to ring. Who was it? What would happen when Meat Neck didn't answer?

Maybe it was DC. Maybe it was his people. Maybe it was Meat Neck's own people with DC's people listening in. Was DC right outside the door? I needed him to have kept his promise. But at this point, if he hadn't, there was nothing I could do. Either he would be there to arrest me or he would let me go. It'd be a test of how bad he felt about a friend being raped versus a stranger, or a test of how much he liked me, or a test of how much he hated his job or wanted to outsmart his bosses or didn't like Meat Neck and didn't want me to suffer for a death that made the world a better place.

The ringing stopped. Silence throbbed in its wake. My mind hit some kind of wall.

The brain delineates the world into survivable chunks. It's not the same as when you're figuring out how to get uptown or saving to afford a trip or trying to get someone to like you. The world becomes very simple.

There was the room. I had to leave the room. There were two doors. I needed to stand, pick one, go. I stood. One door went to the adjoining room, one to the hall.

The hall.

On the other side of the door was either certain death—which would absorb me before I had time to think about it—or freedom.

I opened the door.

No one.

The door closed behind me, and the moment I had just survived collapsed into itself and disappeared. I forgot it immediately.

Stairs and elevator were both to the left. No decision. Walk.

I walked.

I didn't think of the big picture, I didn't look up for cameras. DC could be anywhere, but so far he wasn't here.

I passed the elevator.

Stairs.

A gray column. The hall door closed behind me and that moment was gone, too. I jogged down the stairs, faster as I got lower.

Thirty floors to ground level.

After ten I heard people moving above me and hoped I could run faster than them, but they didn't come down. On seventeen I passed a shirtless man in suit pants smoking. He closed the butt into his hand until he could see my face.

After twelve I broke out in a cold sweat, certain I'd be met by someone with a gun as soon as I opened the lobby door. I had to get out of the stairwell before the lobby.

The mezzanine.

I exited on the mezzanine. The gray world closed. There was a crush of people in office wear mixed with a few in evening. I fully expected DC to betray me and emerge. In some unconscious tribute to horror movies, I gave him a second to come through the same door I just left. He did not. I took this as a message from the universe telling me I had a chance of making it out alive.

I approached the banister overlooking the lobby and my focus expanded.

The pool would have an exit. Stairs in the hotel or along the back wall into the parking garage, but out, either way, out. Then I would untwist myself from the garage up to the street. Two blocks to the subway. PATH to New Jersey. Any train from there.

By the time my mind got me to New Jersey, I was crossing purple rubber mats in the hotel gym.

Mirrors. I paused to check. My hair was tangled but how had that happened? Had it been that way in the bathroom? I was already forgetting what had just happened. I brushed it from my face and saw blood on my cheek. Had it transferred from my hand? I had washed well. I couldn't feel a source or see one. But my jaw ached when I touched it. My knees were red. The right one actually scraped. I only noticed because I felt the skin burning.

The cheek would bruise. I pulled my hair back down, rubbed a finger over the makeup under my eyes, and breathed out.

I was nervous—my first real feeling since I left the room—but it was closer to excitement than fear.

I took a few steps. I pushed open the heavy door into the pool room and a warm puff of chlorine hit me in the face. *There is no rush*, I thought, *I can leave anytime, but I am going to leave right now.*

A LONG, low bell rings out. I swear it enters through my skin instead of my ears. I jump. I think I accidentally hit send, or delete, but the email is still there. It is still light out, but I can't see anything through the windows.

Now the phone is ringing. Unknown caller. I reject the call. The bell is coming from my phone. The bell is the front gate app. It wasn't hard to log in: The information was in the guest booklet. The camera on the gate is a bloom of white. Someone has to be shining a light directly into the camera. It doesn't matter.

There was more to say. Or maybe there wasn't more, but I wasn't done saying it. I stand. The bell again. I hope it is X. I hope it is Justice Bimbo. I hope it is the bookstore employee or my barista or the homeowner or even Walnuts. I imagine it is each.

My heart grows louder. My heart is a metronome. My heart is a stopwatch. My palms are slick. My legs are hot. My mouth tastes like shit. Is this fight or flight? It's too late. I move to send the email as smoothly as I can, as if someone has me in their sniper sights just waiting for a reason to shoot.

But of course they don't. They don't need to.

I buzz the caller in. I desperately don't want to open the door, but it's already over.

It's the only person it can be.

ACT III

I BELIEVE in love. I'm not talking about the lifelong build you see elderly couples opining about. All that stuff about letting your partner be your partner, loving them whoever they become. We all know that's really code for staying together even when he cheated on her or him staying with her when it turns out she's a Disney adult or a home-wrecking psycho. Fuck that. That's a misunderstanding of what sacrifice means. It shouldn't be carte blanche and it shouldn't be random.

And I don't mean the kind of "love" that's all about seeing only the other's good side, those moony couples doting on each other constantly, making saccharine little gestures, celebrating every kind of anniversary, bragging about each other to everyone they meet. I hate that crap.

I'm talking about real love, the kind that is honest and difficult, the kind that requires meaningful sacrifice to seal you together. I mean the kind you only get when you see through each other's bullshit and you *don't* accept it—you call it out and stay together while you each struggle to improve. I believe in the kind of love that hones you each into the best possible version of yourselves, which necessarily means facing the ugliest truths, the stuff the other types of couples ignore, hide, overlook, or forgive.

When you have the kind of love where you see each other for who you really are, the beholding is a kind of technology that counteracts the violence the world perpetrates against you. The kind of love people are shitting on when they say "No one can make you happy until you make yourself happy." Not true. It's like masturbation. You *can* make yourself happy. Technically, yes, it works, but people who say it's cool with them that their partner doesn't know how to make them come are lying. Making yourself happy may be the surest way to get it done, but in my opinion it's for cowards, people who aren't capable of being fulfilled by the love of another person because they've cauterized all the live ends of their soul needed for actual connection. That's not me.

I love love. I'll do anything for it. Well, maybe not anything, but I'll do what it takes. I just forgot that for a few years. This whole story is what happened when I remembered. And if this is how I die, so be it.

DC walks into the cabin.

"I told you not to come," I say.

"It's so good to see you," he says.

Motherfucker. I knew he couldn't help himself. I knew it. Fine. That's fine. I'm ready. I specifically told him not to follow me. I gave him a chance. The words I used were "Believe me when I say, I know what I want and need. Do not follow me."

What he said was "You're selling yourself short. You think you don't deserve to be happy, but you do."

I said, "I do. I do think I deserve to be happy."

He patted me like a child.

"Silly kid, what do you know about your own happiness? One day you will grow up and realize you need me, and I'll be there because I already knew."

I said, "I'm fucking warning you."

He said, "I love it when you cuss."

Cuss. There's something so revoltingly puerile about that word.

So, everything that's about to happen? His fault. Righteous anger vaporizes into pure energy. Light is coursing through my body, excitement. My cells are dancing. In the abstract, I wish he hadn't come, because I don't want him here and can't have him here, and I am not an evil person. In reality, I'm glad he came, because the deal was, if he ignores what I ask for, that's the last proof I need that he cannot be stopped short of death. I will have no choice but to kill him. And right now I really, really feel like killing him.

DC is beaming. I try to smile. He seems genuinely happy. Why do happy people so often look demonic? He clearly has no clue about what's going to happen next. I imagine a red digital countdown clock hovering over his head. Three hours? I give him three hours. It reads "2:59:59." It bobs and blinks when he dips to drop his bag. His head is covered in two days of fuzz. He is wearing blue jeans and a Red Sox sweatshirt, gray New Balance. He's brought a tiny green duffel. *Maybe I'll kill him sooner,* I think, but I don't really consider it. It's just something I say to myself to take the edge off. I'll stick to my plan—it's simple and efficient—and hopefully I'll be gone by midday tomorrow.

"Some place you've got yourself," he says.

What a bullshit thing to say.

I hate the Midwestern tradition of sarcastically complimenting something because you think it's excessive. I get it. It's a fucking rich-guy play pad/end-of-the-world compound. I'm not even staying in the main house. I've colonized one of the smaller guesthouses. The main building is almost as big as my public high school, probably because it has the equipment for pretty every much possible extracurricular activity. There's a dance studio, a squash court, a greenhouse, a movie theater, a library, and an indoor pool. I can't even get started on outside: It's too overwhelming and there are a lot of massive metal sculptures. The guesthouse itself has 5 bedrooms and 3.5 baths and is sparsely furnished in the way that makes sense only to the extraordinarily wealthy.

The property is most conveniently traversed by custom green-and-gold golf carts over rolling paved paths. An extended family could live here comfortably with a full staff. The compound is surrounded by an aggressive security perimeter including a ditch that converts into a moat in case of wildfire or insurrection.

Someone else built it. I'm enjoying it. Seriously, fuck him. Wouldn't it be worse to not enjoy it? And what unacceptable quality about me does it reveal that I'm not in some decrepit off-grid shack? Have you tried walking the fine line of liking and doing only the demure shit that reflects well on you from the point of view of most people? It's exhausting.

God, this guy has an uncanny ability to put me in my brain. He moves closer to me. He reaches out.

"I haven't had time to take a shower yet," I say.

His forehead quirks.

"When did you get here?" he asks.

I shrug.

But then his face relaxes; he smiles.

"It's okay, I used to get jumpy after a job, too. Couldn't let my guard down unless there was someone else around to look out. One time, I swear I didn't sleep for a week."

I want to tell him that it's impossible to go a week without sleep. I want to explain that no, actually, I have filled my time with productivity, women fill their time with productivity, they don't just wait around to do stuff. I want to tell him that having him here "to look out for me" doesn't make me feel better. Women don't feel better alone with one man. They feel better alone.

"I really can't believe you're here," I say. I can. "Do you mind if I take one now? A shower?" I say.

"Of course not. I'll start dinner," he says. He believes this answer is generous.

The quickest way to my bedroom is actually to go out to the deck and down the stairs. But I don't want DC to think I've left the house, even for a minute. I take the interior hall over heated concrete floors. There is art here that should be in a museum—red and black squares in oil, a giant pastel mural of melting icebergs. My room's door opens silently. I wish it didn't. It closes softly, too. My things are a grubby pile hunched in front of the sliding doors. The bathroom fan purrs on as soon as the room's vacuum is broken.

I turn on the shower. Water rains from a perforated black square too high to reach. Switching it on turns the whole room black and the water a luminous purple. I pull myself away. There are clothes in all the rooms, for no one, for anyone. I get clean socks, chocolate-brown label-less alpaca. I choose a plain cashmere sweater. I put on my own jacket.

I lock my bedroom door and leave the house through the sliding glass doors, hop off the cantilevered porch, and skirt the yard, so DC won't see me even if he is looking out the kitchen windows.

I'm exactly on schedule. Now I just need a grave. I look back, but through the window I can see only the golden ceiling of the kitchen, some shadows, a radiating light fixture. There are shovels in the shed at the edge of the yard, buckets, battery-powered lanterns. There's an ATV that wouldn't fit the trails I'm planning to take. For the first time in a very, very long time, I feel entirely unafraid. I carry a shovel into the woods.

Somewhere Justice is reading my words and beginning to simmer. She is pausing to make notes, she is creating a timeline, she is opening tabs "to research," she is thinking about how to pace and polish my narrative into one her listeners can absorb, even when half listening. She is turning me into a legend. I hope I've hit the right tone, I think, but why am I feigning humility in my own head? I know I have. Here's your very own bimbo with a heart of gold to rescue, here's a story about radical sex workers for good, here's a story about the tedium of men. I have given her treasure. She will weave it into lore.

The truth is, I'm proud. Because it wasn't easy to figure out what to write to her. I tried so many drafts where I was less oblivious, more aware. I wrote drafts where I, like her, was both in identity politics' thrall while also being critical of it, wary of the neoliberal wet dream of progress, while secretly hoping it was real, down to choosing the same weak synonym she prefers on her show to avoid saying "crazy." Because honestly, it was hard to stomach writing a politically daft sex worker. And it was also hard because it had to surpass plausibility. It had to be specific.

I had to imagine not only that she would be reading the story but that she would be lifting it up, examining it from all sides, taking it apart and putting it back together. It couldn't be a picture of a machine, it had to be a functional machine.

I tried to make Murder Bimbo be Justice Bimbo's equal, but something wasn't working until I realized that Justice Bimbo doesn't actually want an equal. If she did, that's who she would talk about. She wants someone who never made her own case, someone with enough trouble that she hasn't had the time (but who also doesn't have the intelligence) to rehabilitate herself. She needs someone she believes is lesser, in order to feel charitable and insightful about saying they're the same, in order to save her.

I've listened to every episode she's ever published. I know what turns her on. I know she's just dying for an opportunity to put her money where her mouth is. I had to make that my mantra to get through the stickier parts of the story. My origin story was the hardest part—at least psychologically. At least I didn't have to invent it whole cloth. I took the same story I've told a thousand times, the story I told X when we got together, and tuned it. Those stories are sisters.

The truth is so banal that I've never gotten anyone outside of sex work to buy it. I was a normal book-loving kid who liked school and loved playing all the kid games that didn't involve too much running. For a year I was obsessed with having a sibling and begged my parents to have a baby, but then we got a terrier and that did the trick. Normal.

I did like sex more than other kids cared about it. The summer before seventh grade I had a crush on five or six kids at once. I thought about sex all the time. I knew what it was—at least one form of it—and I was desperate to have it. One of my hobbies that summer was closing my eyes and imagining long scenarios where I got to have sex.

When I told my best friend, she said she didn't feel the same way, but that it was totally normal. I'm still grateful to that best friend and think about her often.

My interest in sex didn't immediately cause problems. I assumed, when I got to high school, everyone else would catch up. I was wrong. It was a hard lesson to learn. People were interested in music, sports, art, but no one seemed into sex. I liked those things, but I saw them as things to enjoy between sex or when sex wasn't socially appropriate, or as a means to meet new people with whom I could have sex.

I started having sex when I was a sophomore in high school. It was fun in the beginning, because I had waited so long. It continued to be fun as I slept with more people. There were a few times that weren't great, either physically or because of some bad emotional stuff. However, those times were easy for me to understand or compartmentalize, and they didn't damage my love of sex.

I evaluated everyone I met, asked them tangential questions, observed them. I knew the kinds of people who I needed to befriend:

People who were also sexual.

People who were attracted to me.

People who could become sexual or attracted to me once we knew each other better.

My senior year, I applied to colleges and decided to attend a large school in a city in another Midwestern state. My parents supported this decision and although we'd always had enough money growing up and they could help with college, I still had to take out a lot of loans, and they weren't able to send money in any regular way for living expenses. That was fine with me. I thought it was normal. But when I got to college it felt like everyone was getting money from their parents and didn't have to work as much as I did. It set me apart.

I wasn't jealous, but I did judge my classmates.

I got a part-time job at a bookstore and worked for a catering company on the weekends, and my second year I moved off campus into a house with grad students because the rent was cheaper, and they were living on less and therefore less likely to use my detergent and leave all the lights on.

Sex became even more fun. Eventually I would call myself a lesbian (yes, that retro word! I still identify this way!), but at that point I didn't have a label for myself. Anytime I tried to think it through, I got confused about whether the label was supposed to be about who I *was* or who I *wanted*. I tried not to worry about it. By then I didn't have to try anymore to find the sexual people. The right ones just stood out. They were always a small percentage, but that doesn't matter much in a school of ten thousand people.

I was happy in college. I didn't care about school as much as I thought I would, but I liked how it felt to live my own life and support myself. When the time came to declare a major, I realized I didn't know what I wanted to do. Because I was acutely aware of how much college was costing, that made me want to barf, so I decided to take leave for a year to figure it out.

I never went back.

Right before I went on leave, I met this woman. You know when you meet someone and immediately know they will be important in your life? Or that's how it feels at nineteen, at least, like fate. She was smaller than me, but always seemed taller. She had a pointed face, hair cropped to her chin, enormous breasts, one green eye and one brown eye, and dyslexia. We met at a concert at school. When I asked her if she lived in the dorms, she laughed at me, touched my cheek.

"Do I look like I go to fucking college?" she said.

I was hooked.

I saw her as often as she'd let me.

Our relationship seemed like it might turn romantic at first. One evening we undressed each other enthusiastically enough, but as soon as we were topless, we discovered the frisson had gone with our shirts. We were both good at sex, but at that moment, neither of us could think of what to do next. We had assumed that because we were both fans of the act and knew that about each other, we could each have chemistry with anyone. "Chemistry" was her word. The sensation went out of my nipples when she kissed me.

I must have looked blank. Something I never did during sex.

"Whoops," she said, "sorry, rewind."

She had the kind of lank blond hair that looked black when wet.

"Sorry," I said.

"No sorry, we're the same," she said.

I laughed. I was so grateful that she was pushing us through the moment.

"Now what?" I said.

I didn't want her to stay exactly, but I felt anxious about her leaving before we had established a new connection of some kind.

"Let's sleep in the same bed," she said, "like sisters."

I agreed. I didn't know what she meant. I didn't have a sister. I brought her a glass of tepid water and she took her shirt off again, but this time in a totally different way.

A few months later we discovered the key was threesomes. The first one happened after a party where we both had "chemistry" with the same guy. He joked that we should both come home with him. He was shocked when my friend said yes. We went back to her place. We had a good time, but from the moment she said yes, we realized we were far more experienced than him, and while that can be charming in many situations, a threesome isn't one of them.

"Next time we should find someone older," my friend said. The guy was in the bathroom with the water running. My friend was finding me a sweatshirt to borrow. She always lent me her most precious sweatshirts, and it felt like a declaration of trust that she would let me take them home to wash.

We talked about a plan, always in that tone of voice that could have been a joke or could have been a sufficient fantasy in itself. The next day we both started looking. The next guy we chose? The sex *was* better.

"We should try online," my friend said, a couple months into things. We had slept with maybe four people at that point. She slightly preferred the people to be men but we both agreed skill and temperament were the most critical factors. And looks, she also really cared about looks.

People were always complaining, about how online dating was full of people looking for threesomes, she said.

"I think that means couples?" I said. And when this didn't register, "The couples are looking for thirds."

But she was right. We were able to find more people online. It was faster and we weren't limited to the contents of a bar or party. Over the next month we were able to find a new person every weekend, and then two a week. As the volume increased, the bad sex became less important.

One night we met someone new, everything went well, we had quick drinks at a bar, went back to his hotel room, and had efficient but solid sex. He showered, then offered us the bathroom. We took turns sitting in the fog while the other showered. He didn't bother us. When we left, the man was gone, and on the desk, he'd left an envelope of cash with our names on it in quotation marks.

"What's this?" I asked. The envelope had a small stack of hundreds.

My friend went gray. She vomited in the waste bin. I took the vomit to the bathroom to flush and scanned my body for feelings. There was nothing gray inside. I felt good. I felt like I had just had sex and now had a wad of cash.

When I returned with the wet bin, my friend was dressed.

"Let's spend it all right now," she said.

"What?"

"All of it, I want to get rid of it," she said.

That was fine with me. The money had been so unexpected, it hardly felt like mine. We got cocktails at the hotel bar and then took a cab to the fanciest restaurant the concierge could recommend. We ordered twice as much as we ate, and still had enough to leave a hundred-dollar tip and take separate cabs home.

I was nervous letting my friend get in her own cab. I thought she'd never want to see me again. I tried to talk to her about it, but she was too drunk to process.

I went home alone and wondered if there was any way to replicate what had happened by myself, while also worrying about my friend. The next morning, I had two texts.

Beautiful night ladies, would love to do it again next time I'm in town.

and

I'm blocking this dude, but totally cool if you want to see him again, you do you. Sorry I overreacted, I'm a freak. I love you!

See? Boring. Nobody likes the truth. Not a lot of conflict, no trauma. I'm a woman who likes sex, and no one ever made me feel that fucked-up about it, so I did what I wanted and also made money. I still like it. People *hate* that. And I know what X would have said if I told her the real truth because I tried it. She thought I was lying. She thought I was repressing more information. She furrowed her brow and looked at me like I was an injured puppy and explained to me that what I thought was my origin story was just the story of the first time I did sex work, that there were circumstances below, there were exploitative systems, there were feelings. I believed her for a little while. I tried to have more sympathy toward my childhood self so that she could have the space she needed to tell me the full truth.

I'm over that now.

I'm still friends with the girl from college. I'm sad I won't get to talk to her anytime soon. Her or any of my friends, but I hope they are in bars and restaurants, gyms, hotels. I hope they're at home in their beds, and that they universally feel a loosening. Meat Neck is dead. Stop clenching your brow. Crack your knuckles. Wash your hair. Take a nap.

I walk through the woods. After so much time in front of the computer, it feels fantastic to walk.

Somewhere X is reading my words, and her heart is beginning to thump in her chest. The danger is a magnet pulling her to me. The truth is, she's a status-seeking name-dropper. And if I am a legend, there will be nothing holding her to her wife anymore. She's probably already backing her electric SUV out of her solar-powered garage.

The main challenge with writing to X was getting over my desire to rant. To go down memory lane about all the fucked-up shit she had done over the years. It still felt hot and fresh. And as I continued the story, I had to routinely sweep myself up, back to the assassination narrative and away from the useless digressions.

So much of love is keeping the connection between you taut—so that if either of you pulls on it, the other can feel it. And keeping the connection taut without being in frequent contact is an art. You maintain it through liking each other's photos or looking at them at the right pace (just after they're posted, then not for a while). You achieve something that will get back to them, and rattle around awhile. It's like fishing. If they FEEL you pulling, they notice it's a hook and swim away. They have to bite into something irresistible, and nibble long enough to get stuck.

And I think I did it.

No one will ever know what actually happened, the real story. That's completely fine with me. I mean, maybe I have *some* hard feelings, but we all have hard feelings about not getting our way. I'm adult enough to know this is how things have to be. One of the costs of the deed I did is never getting credit, not really, not for the way it truly went down, all the layers. As I said before, I'm no stranger to sacrifice. I'll pay that cost. Just right now, I'm a little hyped. I take a deep breath and return to the visualization I've been running on since this whole thing started: me ripped and tan on a beach, drinking a cocktail when X arrives.

God, it was freeing when I finally let myself think of her again. I had to forgive myself for all the time I wasted *not* thinking of her. I thought I was so noble, letting her go. Letting her have the "perfect life" I couldn't provide. But it's never noble to let go of true love. Never. Not even if you think you have a good reason. Not even if the person you love doesn't love you enough to risk her job and life and safety by accusing a rising political star of sexual crimes. Not even if the person you love lures you to a moonlit roof by implying engagement, or at the very least romance, and instead introduces you to a slimy, tepid, weaselly federal agent, who spends the next decade of your life on your ass: following you to work, sending you photos from times you thought you were alone, implying he has tapped your phone, proving he has read your email, and periodically cleaning out your bank account either to flex his power or spend your money, or for no reason at all. That's right.

When someone gives someone else an ultimatum: Who is the dumper and who is the dumpee? Did I dump her because I wouldn't do what she needed me to in order to stay together (her opinion), or did she dump me by placing an impossible condition on us staying together?

When I said no to DC, X said no to me. Then DC said no to me saying no to him. What's worse: What Meat Neck did to me forever ago? Or a rapey, obsessive cop who makes it impossible to get close to anyone without endangering them, too? I shiver thinking of him back at the guesthouse. DC tells everyone he's "tactile" like it's a charming and harmless neurological condition. He's probably palming the candy wrappers I left under my computer, fingering my slippers right now.

The path veers left, then fades. I continue the way it seemed to be heading. I have to break through branches. They get thicker. This is wrong. I back up, turn around, and try another route. This one is clearer. Every step, even the ones I have to retrace, feels like progress. I hope I can find my way back to the house, and I also hope I'm not leaving too clear a trail. I don't really know where I'm going.

I imagine a helicopter passing over. I wonder how visible I am from above. It was spring the last time I was here, but that was years ago, and I remember the forest as less dense, even though the trees were all leafed out then. A bird lands on a branch nearby and a wave of orange leaves showers down. The owner said there are parts of the property no one goes to, no one's ever gone to, when he gave me the tour. I believe *he* doesn't go to them. Probably no one has walked those sections since he bought the land in 2008.

I am getting hot. My sweat smells like onions.

I just need to find one of those spots. Will I know it when I see it? My toes are sweating. It's making me angry. *Imagine the beach*, I tell myself. Imagine that all the reasons you haven't been with X all this time are hurdles, and your legs are growing long. Imagine you and X have long, long legs and are stepping over them all. Now you are holding hands. Now she is yours.

I wipe out.

The terrain requires complete attention and I'm distracted.

Maybe it's my self-confidence. I survey my body, and it seems fine. I get back up. *Don't get blinded by your ego*, I remind myself.

The ex-client refers to the compound as his cabin. This is supposed to be a joke at his own expense that prevents other people from making the joke. A cabin can be a lot of things, but it's not an off-grid luxury getaway across the property from a full-fledged bunker. Or I don't know. How many eschatologically obsessed tech centimillionaires need to call something a cabin before someone adds a new line to the dictionary definition? To be fair, this ex-client is less of an asshole than a lot of that cohort. He's always been nice to me, even after his tastes started skewing a little too Magic: The Gathering x latex for me. Dull x enervating.

At the "cabin," DC is probably making steak, no matter how many times I've told him I'm a vegetarian. I wonder if I'm going to have to fuck him one more time. I hope not. He says he understands that I'm a lesbian. But he says it the way men always do, like it's a compliment to himself and a promise of exclusivity, instead of a prologue to me hating him. One thing is for sure, and that's that he's a little in love with me. No one does what DC did if they're not in some kind of love.

I come to a clearing. I step over a fallen tree into a deep bed of leaves. Beneath it the soil looks black. I nudge it with my foot. It gives. I bite into it with the shovel, then again, then again, then again. Maybe this is the spot. I dig deeper than a foot before I hit clay, and then it is only a few inches thick. There are rocks but no big pieces of shale. This will work. I visualize the black dirt, falling against DC's pale skin. It will feel so good to put him under rock and soil. To walk away while he is getting nibbled by bugs, digested by bacteria, eroded away, broken down into nothing.

There are two stories. The story of X and the story of Meat Neck. And then there's the third story about how I mounted both of those tales before I knew where either was going and corralled them into one perfect, wild saga. But I'll get to that.

I have to walk back into that kitchen, showered, in an hour. I begin to dig.

The plot to assassinate Meat Neck started over the summer. It was a stifling July. I was at a regular's house in Newton that had been purchased with the fortune he had made selling his app (for data) to a megacorp specializing in facial recognition. The regular had only recently become a regular after a friend he wouldn't name referred him to me when he made his windfall.

My friend says you don't mind alternative views, he wrote in one of his first messages. Alternative views. I hoped that meant vaccine skepticism. Fine. I saw him. He was fine. He became a regular.

The regular had a self-replenishing bank account. The regular had a pool. The regular had a dick the size of a horse's and a complicated fantasy about how he, personally, and his horse dick, were sent to earth to breed unlimited horse dicks, which was his contribution toward ending the Black race. The tricky thing was that sometimes he got tipsy and asked me leading questions about whether I thought *he* was actually part Black. And if he was part Black, wasn't his mission "the opposite"?

Anyway, I love sex work. I love it. It's fucking fun. And I'm good at it and it never gets boring. I love how it changes as you do, and how it changes as culture does. I used to think I would get bored of it as I aged, but that's because I assumed I'd always be a twenty-four-year-old seeing office daddies on their lunch breaks. Then I transitioned to girlfriend experience with men my own age. After that I found babysitting anarcho-capitalists who don't really know how to fuck but have pure perversity that has not yet been bastardized by boring porn or disabled by heartbreak. Now there's never a dull day.

This particular regular liked to fuck me with his friends nearby. He thought they were watching. Sometimes they were. They were all in their early twenties. We had already finished sex that day, although he did say he wanted to "go again," and I was pretending like that might happen (repeats weren't part of his virility), floating naked in the pool, when three of his friends came through the house to the back. I'd met them all before. One was always bringing over Tupperware full of his mom's cooking, who had a *heavy* hand with the **Onions**, so they made him eat it outside. One had congenitally white **Eyebrows**, and one had flat growths on his hands (and probably elsewhere because he wore long sleeves and I never saw much of his body) that were dark and ridged like **Walnuts**. I called them these things to their faces, because they called my client 17, for his seventeen-inch dick, which was nine inches long.

"We have an idea," Walnuts said.

"Come out here," 17 said. We were in the pool. It was hot. He pulled my butt into his soft dick.

"It's too hot, come inside," Walnuts said.

17 didn't argue.

"I may need you, baby," he said to me.

"I want to stay in the sun," I said.

These guys had known each other since high school. I don't know how long they had been tight, but in the last year they had started spending a lot of time together, presumably because they had all figured out that they had something in common: neo-Nazi tendencies. They were obsessed with impressing a group of older white supremacists they found online who called themselves the Service. I saw no reason why the group was worthy of impressing, but what do I know about the Nazi pecking order? Someone in the Service had recently told one of these guys that they were "the real deal," which I know because they quoted it all the fucking time. For months they'd been trying to live up to the compliment. So far all they'd managed was defacing the cars of a few Jewish professors and setting some church scaffolding on fire (no one hurt, no lasting damage to church, limited damage to scaffolding, church not even an actual church anymore, just a $1,200/night kitsch rental property). I didn't love what they were doing, but it wasn't like I could stop it, and I did appreciate my vantage point. I was witnessing either some bizarre subcultural shit that would make a great story or the grassroots birth of a political movement.

17 dragged two loungers close to the door so Walnuts could sit in the

shade of the living room and we could lay outside in the sun. I thought there might be another swim in it for me if I stayed, plus I was curious about the new idea. Curious and I liked the way my naked body made the guys visibly uncomfortable.

They were already talking.

It was so hot that I found it hard to concentrate. I caught words here and there, but mostly just fluttered around in my big blank mind thinking my own thoughts about reuniting with X, X's hands, X's feet.

In retrospect, when all this was happening, I was in the early phases of restarting my relationship with X. Which is to say, I had realized I was still in love with her and had figured out she was probably still in love with me, and I was beginning to understand/remember that love is the whole point.

X didn't know about our love yet. I hadn't been in contact with her, per se. We had texted a few years ago when her cat died. Recently, the most I had done was watch her social media content from my fake account, which I'm sure she knew was me, which is why I say "per se." I took the fact that she hadn't bothered to block my fake account as a message, and the message was some version of "You're welcome here." Once or twice, I had even liked things she posted when I was feeling particularly sad, confident, or horny. So weird that all three of those things could motivate me to the same action.

I had been thinking about going as far as emailing her again since that homeless drug addict got illegally searched and arrested in my neighborhood. But it wasn't a good enough reason to reach out to her. I mean, it made me sad for a couple hours, but that wasn't enough. It never made national news.

I thought maybe I could write to her when the neighbors assembled like they owned the man's plight. They seemed insincere, undedicated. I observed, so I could write to her and tell her as soon as something crossed the line into egregiousness. I saw them there gossiping and I judged them for taking up the cause, and for how fast I assumed they would drop it once they were bored. But they actually had stamina. At a certain point, all middle-aged people are looking for a righteous cause with some mileage left on it. Poor homeless dude was like a rotting deer to these people. They initiated a social justice orgy. By the next afternoon there were corrugated plastic lawn signs. By the end of the week there was a website. I could put together some funny commentary on it that would remind her how incisive I was, but all of this was too common to break the silence.

That was too bad. X would love the way I knew X would hate the whole thing. I agreed with her. I hated it, too. I mean, maybe I would have supported it if I thought the bougie neighbors could get the guy released from jail, I imagined explaining to X, but I knew they couldn't. Because they didn't want him released, not really. Which, neither did I. I mean, yes, I did feel bad for the guy. Police are a scourge. But the part of myself I can never let outside was also thinking, *If you get caught for something, that's a failure of your own vigilance, planning, or seriousness.*

The really stupid thing is that while I was going about my life trying to turn the whole mess into a charming excuse for reconnection, it came back around and bit me. I saw my neighbors standing there and thought *Sheeple*. Which led me, I'm ashamed to say, to realize for the first time that I was on a trajectory not altogether unlike the sheeple. Which led me to realize for the first time, too, that I had assumed at some point some cinematic life path options would present themselves to me and I wouldn't even have to think twice about choosing the countercultural anti-sheep option. But that was never going to happen, and I was a dumb fuck for thinking it would. I was just an escort who lived in a nice neighborhood and enjoyed indie bookshops, vacations in the global south, and going to the farmer's market. And because I had no purpose, I also had no partner. Because what person worth being with would ever be with an aspiring upper-middle-class, orthorexic normie? No one. But the one good thing about being sheeple is that you have the opportunity for a redemption arc—or a romance arc, or a revenge arc. For any arc, really, because you can leave your shitty self behind. As soon as I figured that out, I was glad I hadn't wasted my one free reach-out to X on such a vapid cause. I could do so much better.

April became May. In June, I tried to think of reasons to text X, but every time I turned my mind to the project, I found a wall. It had been so long and her life was so stable, I couldn't just slip into her DMs or "accidentally" send her a nude. I needed something big that would grip her long enough for me to make my case. My case being: we're fucking meant for each other.

By July, I hadn't given up, but I had made peace with the possibility that our reunion was years off. Then came the day at 17's pool. That day when I realized that getting back together with X and the kids' new idea had the potential to be the same idea.

". . . that's a dumbfuck idea," Walnuts said. What had I missed? Had it been important?

"Then you come up with something. The Service is actively looking for new cells. They say actively, but no amateurs, we can't fuck around," Onions said.

"Or what, they're going to kill us for a bad audition?" Walnuts said.

"Don't underestimate them, that's all I'm saying," Onions said.

I had missed nothing. I had more time to think my own thoughts. I thought of X's nipples. They were arguably weird nipples, purple and oblong, but exactly alike, symmetrical to a pimple. I salivated.

"That's not how the internet works," said 17.

This was becoming exhausting.

"You're thinking too small," I said.

I just wanted to speed things up with critique.

"She's right," 17 said.

They had convinced themselves of my own intelligence earlier in the summer. Walnuts said I would make a great secret agent. It was a compliment, even if I didn't understand exactly what he meant by it.

Now they were talking about video games. Onions wanted to "just show them" his new skin.

Men never meant what they thought they did. I learned that in sex work. If a man said you would "make a good actress," that meant he thought you were damaged. He thought you were a liar, but a liar who he, for one, could see through, and he was a little bit in love with you, and the love was contingent upon the damage. He believed he knew you better than anyone else and would like to keep fucking you, expected to keep fucking you, even if you did make it as an actress, just so long as you never got a really robust sense of self-confidence. He also thought there was something luminous about you that other people would be able to see if you had a bigger platform.

If a man told you you'd "make a great therapist," you had to cut him off because the work was about to get hella boring. If a man told you you'd "make a great lawyer," that meant he was tired of fighting with you, and angry about it, but in a turned-on way, and also that he believed you were smarter than most men, but since he was smarter than you, your existence proved that he was smarter than most men, which made him more turned on. If a man told you you'd "be a shrewd business lady," it meant he thought he'd overpaid, which meant you were getting old. Which I was. I was getting old. It was harder and harder to see clients who didn't bring up my age, usually still cloaked as a compliment. So, I should really have been helping these guys more than I was or at least listening more intently. But it was hard.

So far, the only straightforward piece of advice a man had given me that I could actually use was that I was never going to make a fuckton of money doing anything where I was the only person producing the labor. He had been a Marxist with a tech company and a mommy fetish.

"Other people have to do the work and the sooner the better. Or machines, but probably people," he said. You have to think about scale.

I was good at arithmetic. I knew he was right.

Not for the first time in my life I wondered if I had ADHD. I assumed these guys thought I could be a secret agent because I was hot and smart. Maybe not as smart as any of them, but smart enough to make them laugh. And they liked to laugh, laughing made them feel like they were protagonists, and these guys, to a one, believed they were born protagonists. They were just protagonists who hadn't found their big idea/adventure/life purpose. Now they were on the hunt for that.

I loved the money in sex work. I didn't love the danger, but whenever

I got through some of it unscathed, I had a feeling nothing else gave me, and that was something. It would take a lot to make me quit. It would take something so dramatic that I couldn't even imagine it.

"Okay, well, if we need something bigger, I have something," Walnuts said.

"Are you going to tell them our idea like it's your idea?" Onions said.

"How long have you been holding out on us?" 17 said.

"Is this the thing I know about?" Eyebrows said.

"Jesus," 17 said.

Onions nodded. Everyone but Walnuts had taken off their shoes. Everyone but 17 already knew what was going on. Now they were tucking their shoes under the shade of the lounger slats. Walnuts was still technically inside the house, leaning against the back of 17's enormous L-shaped leather sofa.

"We abduct Mr. Red and Brown," Onions said.

"Mr. Red and Brown?"

"The politician," Onions said.

"No," 17 said.

"Why? It wouldn't be that hard, they publish his travel schedule online. It would take some research, but he has no protection. We hold him for ransom, or, I don't know, we deliver him to the Service, let them decide."

"No," 17 said.

"Why?"

"Think about it, it's a great idea," Walnuts said. I didn't know why, but the Service didn't strike me as the kind of organization who liked their applicants holding people for ransom. Ransom was déclassé. But that was only half the problem. Mr. Red and Brown was a dumb target.

"He's too high-profile," 17 said.

I wasn't going to get involved, but my mouth had other plans.

"You're wrong," I said. "He's too low-profile, you've got to think bigger."

"Bigger?" said Onions. He looked a little queasy.

"More famous," I said, and because Walnuts rolled his eyes at me, I added, "And you can't abduct him, you should kill him."

"Who?" said Eyebrows, also ashen, but wide-eyed and about to make that turn from sick to thirsty.

"I could do it," I said.

"You could kill someone?" Eyebrows said. His eyebrows climbed to the center of his forehead.

"I could help." I shrugged.

"Why would you do that?" Walnuts said. I could tell he didn't believe me. Maybe he thought I was a narc? *What kind of hooker is a narc*, I didn't ask him. He looked just nervous enough to be dangerous. They all did. I wanted to keep things moving so they couldn't steep in doubt.

"Cash," I said.

This split the group again, all against me, all against my alien desire for cash. But the desire for cash was also banal enough that they trusted it to be true.

"A million dollars," I said.

Eyebrows' eyebrows wavered. 17 nodded. Walnuts rolled his eyes. Onions' face was now slick with sweat, in addition to being green. Two of them came not from exorbitant wealth but from families with enough money not to think a million dollars was a crazy ask, because they also didn't think a million dollars would be enough to live on. They were the kind of guys who would say "You can't do much with a million."

"What are you going to do with a million dollars?" 17 asked.

Never see you again.

"None of your business," I said. I'm sure he thought that a million dollars would mean I kept seeing him but no one else.

"You can't do much with a million dollars," said Onions.

X wouldn't care about the million; she was of the same social class as Onions. She would probably look down on the million.

"How about Meat Neck?" I said.

They loved that. Meat Neck was perfect. They loved to hate him. I wasn't exactly sure why. I wish I were. But this isn't a movie, this is real life, sometimes things just don't make perfect sense. These guys had garbled, nonsensical political commitments. Just like the rest of us. Anyway,

I suspected they also secretly loved him, but saying it would have been social suicide.

That was the moment I realized the perfect symmetry: X had dumped me for my unwillingness to compromise myself for a chance to take down Meat Neck. What better way was there to get her back?

"How?" Eyebrows said.

"Same way: get his schedule, get in there, do it," I said.

"And then what?" Eyebrows said.

"I don't know, use it to impress whoever you thought you were going to impress with Mr. Red and Brown. That's your part to worry about," I said.

17 smiled. Light negging created an important fissure in the group and made me seem like an insider.

I looked at Walnuts. I could tell it was his buy-in I needed.

"She could do it," 17 said.

He rubbed the inch of thigh closest to my labia, and I thought, *Dude, you are not helping my case.*

Walnuts wasn't watching, though.

"I like it," Walnuts said, "maybe."

"What does Seth think?" Eyebrows said.

Seth? I didn't call them by their real names, but I knew none of them were Seth.

That's when a body rose from the couch, another fully dressed man, this one with the face of a rat and the outfit of a professional paintball player. He had been hidden by the back of the sofa.

My tongue turned to cold metal. The federal agent from the roof. My Stalker. Motherfucker *was* under deep cover after all. **DC**. He slid to his feet. It wasn't just his profession that made him a creep, or that he stalked me, or his rat face. Don't ask me how someone can slide to their feet. He did. (I could just see him back in the cabin palpating raw meat.) His delicate movements. The way he thought precision was an act of love, caution, a form of respect. He smiled at me.

I looked at 17. I looked at Seth/DC. I looked at 17. DC had been the friend who recommended me to 17. That's one deeply fucked-up way to spend time with your crush. How long had he been embedded as 17's friend? How long had the kids been credibly plotting a crime to get them noticed?

DC leaned on the couch. He rubbed his eyes, though he clearly hadn't been sleeping. He said nothing, but the guys all interpreted that to mean that he liked the plan. When they turned their heads, he twitched at me.

My phone buzzed.

Unknown number.

Haven't seen you naked in a while, damn.

The man was a shark's mouth.

I put the phone down. It buzzed again.

I love my job.

I didn't really consider leaving. I probably should have. No doubt he was going to try to fuck me over. So what? We all get arrested for attempted first-degree murder. Just on principle I couldn't let that happen.

I wasn't going anywhere.

I texted him back: **I love MY job.**

Sometimes the fastest way out of something is through. X had an abiding hatred of Meat Neck. She'd been famous for it before he was famous. This was the perfect opportunity to impress her, rid the world of a heinous asshole, make a shit ton of money, and start a new life. All I had to do was figure out how to pull it off, how to keep the guys interested until it was done, and how to do the whole thing without getting killed or arrested by DC.

I love a challenge.

I TAKE a whiff of mountain air, hoping for petrichor and coming up with wind and distant diesel.

DC isn't a heavy guy, but dragging him even a short distance would be exhausting. I want to dig as much of the hole as I have time for now. It's hard, though. The rhythm is therapeutic, the smell fresh, the sounds of metal slicing through dirt so sharp and wet and consistent, it's almost meditative. I start to feel drowsy. I wish I had remembered to bring some water. I lean the shovel against my hip and stretch my arms out.

He could have walked a different direction off that rooftop with X and me, too. He could have forgotten me, or checked in now and then, or reported me to someone whose jurisdiction I fell under. Instead, months later, once I had nearly forgotten his face and my relationship with X was beginning to fray, he found my ad and booked an outcall. He reported great progress against Meat Neck by his department. He inflated his job's importance. I called bullshit. We fucked. That was the least irritating part of it, because I was used to fucking guys I didn't like very much. He didn't set off any alarms or seem like he would become a stalker. But then he tried to convince me to take Meat Neck to court again. I said don't call me. Ever. I told him I was blocking his number. I refused to return his money.

"I like you," he said.

I knew then he was going to be a problem. Now I would finally correct it.

I left 17's house flush with an optimism that kept sliding into rage. I felt tall walking home alone. I hadn't been in my apartment for ten minutes before DC rang the buzzer. I met him downstairs.

"Let's go for a walk," I said. Once I knew he had successfully found a way into this episode of my life, the shift to condescension was effortless. My fetid feelings for DC had rapidly fermented. Which is to say, they were still disgusting, but now they were more interesting and complex, intoxicating.

"Surprised?" he said.

"You got me," I said.

"Happy surprised?" he said.

"Excuse me?"

"Originally, I just thought it would be a good way to hang out. You get paid. We get to see each other. But now we're killing two birds with one stone!"

He smiled. He tried to frown. He smiled. DC was giddy. We turned up Mass Ave.

"Come on," DC said. He put his hand on my lower back.

I wiggled out of it with more revulsion than I would have liked to reveal. No one else was on the sidewalk. It was a clear day. The cement radiated heat.

"This was because you wanted to hang out," I said.

"I could have brought in any girl. I could have helped them plan a version without a girl!"

It enraged me that he thought I was a pawn in his scheme.

"It didn't seem like they had any real plan yet," I said.

That was a mistake. He grinned.

"No?" I said.

"But now they do. And I can make it happen," he said.

He put his hand on my shoulder. The light had changed. I counted to three before stepping out from under his hand and into the street.

"Come on, I'm not that bad. If I hadn't been there today, you would have been all in," he said. "I just caught you off guard."

"So, explain this to me. Finally, after all this time, you are no longer trying to prosecute Meat Neck. Now you want to kill him?" I said.

He looked like he was trying to figure out what he was allowed to say.

"Times have changed?" he said.

"So, you're here to . . . ?"

"My remit has always been to control his influence," he said.

"You've been doing a great job so far," I said.

"Ouch."

I stopped walking. A flock of grad students exited a six-story building and walked past us. I stared at him.

"Fine," he said. "The lawsuits didn't work. Obviously. And we've been trying to blackmail him, but it's impossible. His followers don't care about anything. We were the ones who released that 'soft rape' clip, and people acted like he gave everyone a free car."

He wasn't wrong.

"This is your job? Not your creepy side hobby? Your boss knows you're working with these guys?" I said.

He shrugged. "Not yet, not technically. But he will. They've been looking for an opportunity and now I have one. I'm already in and I can make sure the job gets done."

"And you're just telling me all this—you're allowed to tell me all this?"

"Who are you going to tell? And frankly, would anyone even believe you?"

"Harsh."

"No, I'm the last person to underestimate you, but you have to admit, there are factors working against you here."

I didn't respond. What was there to say?

"Look, it's good news. We get to work together on this, it's like we're a little team," he said.

"And then you're going to sell me out. And you get to be a secret agent, and I go to jail or get killed by secret service," I said.

"Meat Neck doesn't have secret service, he has private security."

"You know what I mean."

"There's no reason anyone has to even know you're involved. The most important thing is that the job gets done. Someone's going to get in trouble, but it doesn't need to be everyone, and it definitely doesn't need to be you. Who would even believe you got involved in this kind of thing anyway," he said.

Everyone, I didn't say. Because it was true, right then, but I needed it not to be if we were going to succeed.

"Are you still mad?" he said.

"Yes," I said, "but let's get something to eat."

People have accused me of it before, but I'm not a liar. A liar is a person who makes things up. I don't make things up. I tell the truth at whatever cost. I tell the truth even if it means I have to edit a story for people to get the important parts. I pay attention to what people hear and adapt the story so that they hear the pertinent thing, and don't get tripped up on irrelevant flashy details.

It's a skill it took me years to hone.

I wish it weren't like this. I wish you could tell an objective story. But we listen to every story while shuffling through a deck of premade narrative arcs in our minds, and as soon as it begins to fit one of them, we drop it in and stop listening. We come to no new conclusions. We do not learn. That's just how it is. I think everyone figures this out at some point. I just noticed it a little earlier than some people and it bothered me more, getting misunderstood, so I started working on it the way some kids work on baseball or flirting.

There are so many silky influencers these days lecturing on manifesting a new life. But I did all this the old-fashioned way. I took a long, hard look at my talents and network and asked myself how I could combine these matrices into a brand-new, better life.

The guys threw themselves into planning the assassination. I started going to 17's almost every day because he paid me whether or not he'd scheduled it, and I was into the plan. The thing about the guys was that every single one of them thought the reason Meat Neck had not yet been assassinated was because no one as smart as them had ever tried. They believed their attention was the most precious resource in the world.

I decided the best approach with DC was to try for amnesia about the stalking, and if I couldn't get to amnesia, I could tell myself that he just had poor professional skills, the way so many psychologists say incels have poor social skills. I tried to think of him as a friend. He was the only one in the group who was about my age. He did seem to be the smartest of them, which wasn't saying much. He was the only one who wasn't a neo-Nazi, which wasn't nothing. I tried to practice liking him. Plus, the more I saw him at 17's, the less he surprised me in my personal life. Still, all I was able to muster was a very thin layer of politeness that could be scratched off with the slightest irritation and had to be constantly, painstakingly reapplied with a litany of excuses.

The guys talked about redundancies and the importance of intel. I thought they were overthinking it. They were trying to build a spiderweb of contacts on a whiteboard to get to Meat Neck. I called the Curator, who I'd worked with once, but who inexplicably made my skin crawl, and she hooked it up.

"Nah, he's always looking for new girls. It's harder for him now with the press. Can I connect you? He would be so happy with me if I did that, literally," she said.

"Totally," I said.

I texted the number. A guy "named Pablo" responded. He said he was a friend of Meat Neck's. I wouldn't tell X about the skin-crawling or the simplicity. For X, the Curator would need to be beautiful enough to remind her that I was desirable, but different enough from X that her jealousy wouldn't turn into anger. This was about when I started putting together the story I would tell X about the whole thing. It became a hobby. Every time the kids began talking about whatever guys talk about I would click over to scripting the story for X.

Meanwhile, I kept texting Pablo. I was 98 percent sure that Pablo was just Meat Neck. If not, he sure had a lot of Meat Neck's dick pics on his Galaxy. I wanted to keep the contact fresh, but it was also alluring to have Meat Neck's number. I would see him doing a press conference and buzz his phone, hoping to catch him reading my message on TV.

The guys moved on to murder weapons. I started planning my exit strategy. Even that first day, at the pool, I had known I would need a way to get out, something that would make me untouchable without also leaving me poor. I started withdrawing cash, collecting burner phones, researching non-extradition countries and how to get to them. But I had no unified strategy for a while. I had no idea how to write a plausible public apologia.

I didn't know how I was going to get rid of DC. I didn't believe the guys would go out of their way to volunteer me to the cops if they didn't have to, but if an insider turned them in, they would probably throw me under the bus to save themselves.

The answers didn't come all at once, but I found them in swaths. One day, 17 and Eyebrows were watching *Citizenfour* about Edward Snowden and how he leaked military information. In order to protect himself from being disappeared, Snowden calls Glenn Greenwald and gets him to fly to Hong Kong, where Snowden tells him his whole story, after the fact, thus transforming himself from a traitor into a whistleblower. I thought, well, that could work.

I knew it was a good idea because it sounded like one right away. Every time I had a question, the answer would present itself. Could a woman get away with what Snowden did? Not exactly. But one could get away with a variation of it. Could a woman like me get away with the variation? No, but I could use a different persona. Would a prominent centrist journalist fly across the world to take my statement? No, but a podcast host with a boner for justice and a neoliberal crush on grassroots organizing would respond to a street-smart queer sex worker in danger.

I began to write my story.

Of course I didn't actually *write* any of it. Instead, I took it for walks with me, unrolling a piece at a time of what I would say happened. Sometimes I would reach a section I couldn't figure out, or a problem I couldn't solve. That didn't faze me. I'd take just the problem with me every day, trying to unknot it as I shopped for produce, returned library books, got fucked by fifty-year-old dudes on long lunch breaks. I didn't write it down, because I knew the story had to be simple. Anything that I needed to write down to remember wouldn't be convincing. Most important, I had to find a way to translate collusion with white supremacists to assassinate Meat Neck into an irresistible love story for X. Talking to her was an exercise in needle threading. I had to be sexy, but not to the wrong people. I had to be political, but could not actually talk about my local political engagements, because she would surely find fault with them. I had to be hot, funny, adult, healed, and alone-as-fuck without being slutty, depressed, embittered, or lonely. I had to break the story into chunks for Justice Bimbo that would naturally lend themselves to episodes, with dramatic tension, cliff-hangers, and just the right amount of pathos in the right places. For X, I had to dangle just enough story that she stayed curious, protective, and a little horny for me. I knew I could figure it out.

I am still impressed with how quickly I read X when we met. I was so fucking young, but, still, I did it effortlessly. Actually, I did it with the subterranean effort of years of practice that were invisible to me at the time.

X's family occupied that ubiquitous and revolting seam commonly called "upper middle class." And like many of their peers, her parents raised her to believe she was "middle class." She always felt left out as a child, which she attributed to her unnamed queerness—then years later, after same-sex marriage passed and increasingly fewer people in liberal strongholds could imagine homophobic parents, she told people it wasn't her queerness that set her apart, it was just her intelligence. Maybe that was true, and she discovered it as she aged. I don't know. X is queer and X is brilliant. Both are more off-putting than the country admits.

X is unlike anyone else, and she wants people to know that, but she also wants to pass at times, and fool people at times, and always be able to claim people treat her poorly, because she is so noticeably unlike others. I found this little human quagmire at the center of her stony facade endearing.

When I met her, she had the dogmatic politics you can only have if you're a convert, the contempt for the upper middle class you can only have if your parents still live there and love the shit out of you. She had never had to pass as rich enough to take seriously because she'd always been rich enough to take seriously.

I skewed my biography accordingly.

I implied my family was "lower middle class." I fed her a sad backstory about my ignorant parents and let her walk me through breaking up with them. I did not actually break up with them! I reminded her that to poor people, the upper middle class (to which I outwardly agreed she did not belong) seemed wealthy. That gave me the basis I needed to show her my political ignorance. Politicizing me was a drug—to both of us. It forged us into an imbalanced dyad, leader and supplicant, top and bottom. I loved it. It was sex and devotion and truth in a world full of lies about equality. The deeper I believed, the more of her political education I devoured and regurgitated, the more I became hers. Which is why it was such a betrayal when she called a federal agent. You can't simply transfer vulnerability. You can't show up with a stranger on a rooftop and tell your girlfriend that if she loves you, she owes a man everything.

Was it a test?

I knew saying no to him would slit open my relationship with X, pop our seal, and she would be free to consider leaving. But I couldn't give her what she wanted. I failed the test.

For a year after our breakup I could not understand why she would ever have faith in some fed to actually listen to a sex worker, to actually take down Meat Neck, to not fuck me over. Then I watched her fall in love with some drip, get married, take a job at an NGO, start appearing as the gay face on panels with middle-of-the-road Democratic spokespeople. I realized that *she* wasn't a true believer. She was just a queer in her early thirties, about to return to the politics her family raised her in.

Now that, I could have survived. I could have survived her turning out to be someone else. I could have survived her abandoning the same politics she had supposedly inculcated me in. I could have survived the loss of the greatest love of my life, despite the fact that her betrayal and her real character did nothing to diminish the heartbreak.

But. There was another cost to saying no to DC on the rooftop. He hated hearing no even more than she did. I was the key that unlocked his life's obsession, or maybe I was just a girl he could push around. I became both. I don't know which came first. Without X in my life, there was nothing stopping DC from permanently attaching to me.

After the first date, he booked me under a fake name. This time we didn't fuck. I refused. He used his time to try to win me over—he tried to convince me that my story with Meat Neck was dramatic enough to make a difference. But I could tell he didn't know what he was doing. If he could bring me on board, he might be able to impress someone or even get promoted, but he wouldn't be able to protect me and he wouldn't be able to bring Meat Neck down. The longer X and I were apart, the less chance DC had. I thought he would see this and give up.

Finally, I convinced him that it wasn't happening. He agreed to believe that it wasn't happening *yet*. He said he would be there for me "as a friend" "until I was ready." I tried to say no thank you. I tried everything to get rid of him. Everything. Being polite and honest, being brutally honest, being cruel, hurting him, pleading with him to go, scaring him. But he proved himself to be every kind of leech, a male shape-shifter incapable of absorbing his own rejection.

I told X about all of it. For the first year after our breakup we still talked all the time. Then, after she met her wife, we talked less but still checked in sometimes. Every time I brought him up, she grew quiet. It was the kind of quiet that felt like anger, though all of this was over the phone so I couldn't really be sure. She would ask me questions about how I responded to him, looking for ways I might have encouraged him, pointing out instances when I could have been harsher ("more clear") or nicer ("less combative if you really want to get your point across"). I thought she would volunteer to call him, tell him to leave me alone. I hoped she would threaten him! But she no longer loved me in any kind of way that made her feel like hurting people. Finally, one day she interrupted my latest story about how he had done "research" on how easy it was to find my nudes online to tell me that if it got bad enough she "knew my friends would help."

My friends. She was shutting me down and she was telling me we weren't even friends anymore. If we weren't friends, I said, then she shouldn't be talking to me, because that meant we were just "exes" and how would her wife feel about that. She said I was right. We hung up. When she messaged me in the middle of the night a few weeks later, I ignored it.

Things with DC got worse. I told him to leave my nudes alone and he apologized. He said he had misunderstood how to help me. He would try again. Engaging with him felt like it wouldn't solve anything, but I didn't know what else to do because he was not going away.

He said we had a deep connection. He said he'd learned so much from me. He said he knew it wasn't reciprocal, but he was kind of in love with me. Each time we followed the same pattern: I tried to get him to leave me alone, he argued, I tried to get him to leave me alone, he threatened to have me arrested for sex work, I cried, he apologized and said he wanted to be my friend, he just wanted to help me leave sex work and have a better life. The cycle grew shorter and shorter. Pretty soon we had it truncated down to: I say no to anything, he threatens to have me arrested. This did, actually, scare me. Prison has always scared me: the foreclosure of choices, claustrophobia. I began to have panic attacks when I saw him. Panic attacks when an unknown number appeared on my phone.

I consented to him calling us friends. Behind the scenes I was still hoping to come up with a new idea when he showed up at 17's and caught me off guard.

All through July and August, DC and I spent a lot of time together. The stretches I hated most were the long swaths of conversation or the times he polluted my alone time by insisting we read together. Sometimes he would speechify about unrelated topics: blockchain, for instance. I would use that time to run through my story for Justice Bimbo or to think about X's gnarled hands ripping open my body. In a sexy way. Sometimes he'd talk to me about his ideas of the world and I would recommend Marxist tracts or progressive writing—sometimes ones that X had originally recommended to me. Pretty soon I discovered he was really reading the shit I suggested, so I would then have to go and read the articles I'd only heard of. One night, while I was scoring tofu, he pulled out a dog-eared copy of some history of the progressive moment and told me, with tears in his fucking eyes, that I had changed his life. I knew what he meant, because, I, too, had once been a teary-eyed young person, politicized by someone whose intelligence I'd overestimated, just because I was hot for them.

I stupidly, briefly thought that I could turn that feeling into true romantic love and use the love to make him do what I wanted (leave me alone) and that, *that* is why I started fucking him again.

As much as possible I tried to stay close to DC at 17's. I sat next to him on the couch. I followed him into the kitchen when he went. I wanted him to know that I didn't feel like being apart. When we were alone together, I initiated sex as quickly as I could. I was sleeping with him for free, or, as he called it, "for fun." I inadvertently created a point system in my own brain for keeping track of the attention I owed him. If he was all paid up, I didn't have to text him back in the middle of the night when he just wanted to talk. I felt I needed to keep him happy, so he would not suspect that I was working on a plan to bring him down—even though there was not yet even an inkling of that plan.

For a brief period, he did sort of grow on me. The disgust faded, all the intense feelings did. They were replaced by a bland hum, not unlike the sound of a refrigerator, which dulled everything he said and calmed me. I started hearing DC in the most generous ways. Part of this may just have been that it was refreshing to be on his side, or to have him on my side, for once. He was definitely less annoying when he was getting his way. His banal stories of growing up in Indiana sounded sweet. His popularity in high school seemed to reflect a better version of America where teenagers valued the right things. Even his extreme caution, which had never seemed sexy, started to feel perverse in a way, and therefore erotic. It wasn't erotic to me, but I thought it might be to someone else, and they could have a nice relationship, if he could get his claws out of me, which I knew, to him, seemed like my claws in him.

I wasn't fooling myself. I knew I was just in a weird spot. If the situation had been different, I would have gotten on the apps and found a girl to have a fling with. But DC was right there, and expanding my social circle in the moment seemed like a bad idea, and somehow fucking a woman and risking romantic feelings felt like cheating on X in a way that playing around with DC just didn't.

In my head, my temporary non-hatred of DC was useful. It would make our inevitable breakup stick, because it would be a real breakup. I had finally given him the chance he wanted, and he would have to see that we didn't work together and let it go. I would like to say I was confident enough to trust that DC would just follow me, as he'd promised. But I felt I needed to shore up his allegiance. I worked on it. All I had to do was fuck him well, and with enough vacant, well-timed glances to help him believe I could be in love with him, too. And he did. He told me he knew it was difficult for me to admit how he respected me so much, my bravery, and also that our being together didn't negate my previous identity as a lesbian, he said. "Negate" was the word he used and the word that told on him. Ha. He was so sure of his theory I could have responded in any way without tipping him off. At first, I did nothing, but eventually I fueled the fire because I was bored. I did this by insulting him, and with dramatic exits, as if I were overcome with emotion. It was fun.

I spent a little over a week listening to him vomit his life story. Middle-class parents, happy, he thought, until he went to college and then discovered they'd been staying together just for him. He went home for Christmas freshman year and they had actually set up home again, just for the holiday, because they thought it would feel more normal for him. He had always hated lies. Something about the whole thing really messed him up. He didn't know if it was the fact that they were lying or the fact that they didn't know him well enough to understand how much he hated lies. I didn't say, *Some people would kill for parents who cared how they felt.* Whatever the reason they'd done it, he swore he would never live with them again, even for a holiday. I didn't say, *Maybe they were taking a vacation from their breakup, maybe it was nice for them to spend Christmas together.*

He knew he had it much better than a lot of people, he agreed, but that experience with his parents really taught him about human fragility, and as soon as he got back to college, he gave his coat to a homeless man. On principle, he didn't buy a new one until the next year. I didn't ask what principle that was. I frowned and nodded and thought about X with her wife drinking espresso in their kitchen in the morning, which brought light tears to my eyes, then I flexed my foot, which stretched my calves, which were criminally sore, and that kept the tears alive.

Occasionally I would interject stories of my own—either fictitious or about other people, screwed by corruption, little guys doing the right thing, following all the rules, and still finding themselves destitute or incarcerated because the state deemed them unfit and ground them into a paste. These would work him into a lather. Sometimes I calmed him, and sometimes, to build the facade of our relationship, I argued. If you want a relationship to seem real, you have to include some arguing.

Have you ever been so angry with someone that you will argue against all their points, even if they start agreeing with you? Even if they don't start agreeing with you, but they start generalizing their view into something bigger and bigger, and more and more universally "good," so that you have to backbend to find something you disagree with? Have you ever had to pause in an argument, as if from emotion, only to hear the fuzz of the room warming and infiltrating the holes of your face, putting you to sleep, because you've been arguing for so long, for so, so long, that you have to take a catnap while pretending to look out the window, as if sad about the new distance between you and the person with whom you are arguing? X taught me the art of the twenty-four-hour impassioned plea. I perfected it after her with other girlfriends. It felt good to sling it over my body like armor and take it into the battle with DC.

I knew it was working when he said he needed to take a break, and I told him we needed to finish the conversation. When he said we could come back to it tomorrow, I told him I would feel abandoned if we did that. He got misty and looked more in love with me than ever.

I apologized for our weak, tired bodies, and I apologized for being so "messed up" and "fragile" and traumatized by the world, which had taught me, through lack of love and my own fucked-up brain chemistry, that when people stopped arguing it meant they didn't love you anymore.

"When this is done, I may need a little time alone to recover," I said.

"I know you're afraid. I'm not going to desert you," he said.

Whatever death grip "the fear of abandonment" has on Gen X/Millennials is a great scourge that will one day be studied. What the fuck does it even mean? So much bad stuff is done to assuage it, or to justify asking for it to be assuaged.

"I'm serious. Just to decompress. When I'm ready, I'll call you," I said.

"You have time to think about it," he said.

I should have said "I'll think about it." But, no, that probably wouldn't have worked.

"I already know," I said.

"I know you think you do," he said.

I was quiet.

"I love you?" he said.

Maybe I took it too far, I don't know. After a lifetime of research, I'm not sure there's a way to deflect a man who doesn't want to be deflected. But it's true, I did encourage DC, and so I shouldn't have been surprised in August when he dished us both up some vegetarian roti and said he had a big announcement.

"Once this is over, we can be together," he said.

"No?" I said. "I'm leaving. We all have to split up. You'll get in trouble if you're caught with me."

He inhaled. He blushed.

"I'm quitting my job. I'm leaving with you," he said.

Fuck.

I ran through all the ways I knew how to get rid of a man: be direct, be indirect, hurt him, distract him, disappear. I had tried them all, plus combinations of most of them, on DC and they still hadn't worked. This man had now been following me for almost a decade. Not only did he have the skill to do it, the connections to get me arrested or probably disappeared, he also had ten years of minute knowledge of my behaviors. No matter how good I was at cooking up a plot or convincing the world to believe me, he had an advantage. In many ways, I believed he did know me better than I knew myself. It was obvious, I had to get rid of him once and for all. It was no longer just about sex work; now it was about colluding with a terrorist organization to commit first-degree murder, which was fine, but I didn't want to rely on narrowly outwitting him for the rest of my life. Best-case scenario, he didn't turn me in, but he haunted me everywhere I went. My debt to him for keeping me free would be literally unlimited. No. I would rather be dead.

He had to go. He had to be totally and completely gone.

It was a simple idea. It went something like this: Hey, maybe you're overthinking this. Maybe the answer is something you've been thinking of already, more of the same, a variation on a theme, built into something else you're going to do. Why master a skill just to use it once? Murder. I remember lying there, looking at his fluttering eyelids as his body tried and failed to get to REM, and in that moment I saw his beauty.

I think all people are beautiful, that's probably why I can be a sex worker. I don't mean I'm attracted to them, I just mean in my mind, I am able to pivot around their visage or self or whatever beautiful part they have until I see it clearly, like a Magic Eye coming into focus. Once I see the beauty, the sympathy can flow. If I took one mental step to the side, though, I could see his face stop moving. I could imagine I was not next to a person but a corpse. Maybe not even a full step. Maybe that thought had been there all along. Maybe the beautiful parts of all the people I had seen before were just their vulnerabilities, which was the same as their death. Maybe I would be very good at delivering them to a permanent state of that. Maybe.

Maybe I'm a killer. Maybe *that's* who I am. If I can kill Meat Neck, I can kill DC. Just do one, then the other.

The answer felt fresh and good. I let it stand.

The next part, to be honest, was googling "how to get shredded in eight weeks or less," because (1) there wasn't going to be a lot of room for error on these murders, (2) both men I was planning to kill were substantially bigger than me, (3) in one case, at least, I was going to have to dispose of a body, and (4) the real "why" behind the whole thing called for sexy-as-hell muscles.

I gave myself a moment (afternoon) just to revel (masturbate) in the eventual outcome of my plan. I hovered between—I'm still hovering between—thinking of myself as an evil genius and a simple carnal beast. But both are good, so maybe I can be both.

And I would get ripped. To ensure my survival, but also because I happened to know X has a thing for shoulders.

After that, everything became easy. Or, not easy, because it took a lot of work, but the work felt like something I had to show up for and practice, rather than something that could undo me or the plan. I had the most beautiful two months of my life so far. In the morning, I trained for an hour, showered at the gym, then went home to accomplish one or two tasks toward the erasure of my life. In the afternoon, I would go to 17's to fuck, then I would go for a run in his posh neighborhood, return, and shower. Then DC and I got into the habit of cooking dinner together while the rest of the guys played video games.

I worked on the story for Justice Bimbo, who would turn me into an icon. After all, when you took a step back, I was just a random sex worker in league with neo-Nazis to stab a politician. You have to weave a special yarn to get the feminists and liberals and progressives and anarchists to align against the state and whoever else would at some point come to get me. But in the right hands . . . in the right hands the story would be irresistible.

I worked on the story for X, who wouldn't be charmed by millennial job quests and government assassination montages, but would need a story that made her feel smart. She would also have to see my bloodthirst as a mirror of her own. No one likes bloodthirst unless it mimics their own. And DC had to be a sweet guy: respectful, better than other guys for the disgusting combination of reasons that X prided herself on "hating men," and if she found out I had actually fucked him, she would be revolted. I had to walk a fine line. He had to be safe and kind enough to be around, but not so safe and kind that he could encroach upon what she believed was her own due, my body. Plus, even though she had ignored me when I needed help dealing with him, she'd feel vindicated to discover that I had been exaggerating his behavior, or that I had been underestimating my own ability to handle him.

That was okay. That was kind of charming. I hate to say it, but her jealousy made me happy. X kept me going. X was how I found energy after twelve hours with the guys and three more hours with DC. All the best motives are simple and sturdy, I guess. That way they can peal around your body when you call on them and, unexpectedly, they can wake you up, calm you down, or bang you into service. And my motive was as simple as it could get. It was the fucking dumbest, most classic why of all time. It shone a light onto every other aspect of the plan—a series of mechanisms I thought had been brilliant, complex, well-tuned—and revealed that below them all was one big, beating organ powering the rest, nothing smart, just dumb meat, and that dumb meat was ardor.

MY WATCH beeps. I've cleared a hole about the size of DC's body. Maybe it's more of a dent. It needs more work. But there's time and I'll come back refreshed. I was scared I would be bad at killing people. Nice to find out I'm not. Turns out, killing people is like getting fired or breaking up with someone: The sickening part is the anticipation. Once you get to the action, there's too much to do to have many feelings. It's a nice change, actually.

The path is easier to find now that my eyes have adjusted to the darkness. I stop to move a big branch off the trail. DC is probably looking for candles to light. The good thing about him is that he prefers companionable silence to conversation. He thinks it feels deep.

Silence isn't deep. We just think it is because we're filling it in with our own shit, then believing our partner agrees with us. X and I were just the opposite. We were awake for two years almost constantly, talking. Our entire lives together were annotated. So many conversations were woven into one another that we could hop seamlessly between them, so that by the end, we were able to argue while also agreeing on something else, while planning dinner, while telling a story. Our love affair was a lens that made the world appear in minute detail for our analysis. That was a balm for the loneliness of my childhood. Isn't that the most effective love potion? She didn't even need to really know about my actual childhood to heal my childhood.

If I had known how rare that was, I don't know, I may not have let X go. It is so hard to wake up alone with your thoughts. It's hard to try to talk to someone and find dead ends early in every thought process. It's depressing to watch the world dull and blur because there's no one there to open it up with. I do believe if I had held on to her, I could have anchored her as she was.

Her wife changed her into a neolib tool. I don't blame the wife. I like the wife! I have come to like the wife. But I could have kept X. I could have.

The house smells like thyme. DC has turned on Cat Power. Unbearable. It's hard to limit my shower to a quick scalding scrub, but I do. It really does feel like I'm standing in a peaceful, warm rain. I will come back after all this and take a nice long soak.

He has made some kind of tofu stroganoff. It smells rich and heavy without smelling like meat. My hunger has passed into a bodily deficit I have never felt before. I hate soy trying to be meat. See, this is what I mean, this is the kind of thing in a normal relationship I would be expected to give him credit for. He's trying. But he's not stupid, so is this really trying? The spinach does look good, it's a deep green velvet tongue in a brown pool of its own juice.

IT HAD been easy, when the day finally came. DC convinced his superiors they would blow the operation if they came too close. That was fine with them, they didn't really care about busting the guys. They had been letting DC "monitor" them to get him out of their hair, but when he happened to come upon a credible opportunity to kill their target, they were stuck. They needed Meat Neck dead and the blood on someone else's hands.

There was a gala happening at the hotel when I arrived, and I saw Meat Neck there, talking to some B-list celebrities. I saw him and he saw me. He waved. For a second, I thought he recognized me. I was a little nervous to go to his room, but I translated the nerves into anger and went up anyway. I waited there for half an hour. Meat Neck arrived exactly when he said he would. He had recognized me, but only from the photo I had sent "Pablo." He complimented me, and it. I wondered if he had forgotten our entire encounter because he had been wasted at the time. He hadn't seemed wasted, but what did I know. Or was it possible he'd forgotten it because it was so out of character that he'd built a sarcophagus around it in his memory and tucked it away? Or he had done it so many times since then, seen so many women who looked so much like me, that he had to frequently quell a little voice suggesting he might know someone or give himself away?

It was nothing like the time before. He smelled different. Even his voice was deeper. He was nice. He offered to take a shower. I said he didn't need to. Honestly, he seemed tired. He told me he was planning to get out of politics. He told me his daughter said she was worried about the world he was making for her own future daughter, and that that shouldn't have gotten to him, but it did. He wasn't sure she was right, but he had doubts. Doubts were enough.

He paid me. He tipped me a stingy 10 percent, but who cares. Maybe he meant to give me another tip after we fucked. We fucked. He asked if I wanted room service. He told me I could leave whenever, and that he'd like to book me again if he was back in New York anytime soon. He asked me where I was from. I told him the truth. When he sat down on the bed to order the room service, I stabbed him in the gut.

DC wasn't in the hall when I left. He wasn't on the mezzanine. He wasn't in the gym. I didn't see him on the street or near my car. I thought, for just a little while, that maybe I had had the world wrong. Maybe Meat Neck would have reformed and DC had heard me when I told him I needed to be alone.

"THIS STUFF isn't too bad. I thought I would miss meat, but so far I don't," DC says.

That does make me feel bad. A man's last meal shouldn't be tofu stroganoff, no matter how awful he is. Oh well. Last meals are arbitrary. We all die, right?

"I have something to show you when we're done," I say.

"Really?" he says.

"In the woods," I say.

He is curious.

"It's a sauna, but I don't know if it's working," I say. I chew a whole glass of ice because he hates it, then I eat the entire meal because I'm hungry and it's not bad. I try to focus on my plate or to gaze, as if thoughtful, onto the moonlit deck behind him. It's a cloudless night. I catch DC with the wistful grin of someone who thinks he's finally met the pliable love of his life. *I'll get the sauna working*, I know he's going to say.

We wash the dishes before we go. Or he does. I'm not going to waste the last few minutes of extra hands in the house.

When the kitchen is clean, I make us both cocktails. Mine a martini, his a penicillin. I add a float of Laphroaig on top.

"Are you trying to get me drunk?" he says.

"I think there's a hatchet for the sauna in the mudroom," I say.

"Aw, you brought the honey-ginger syrup?" he says.

"Of course."

"For me?"

"Well, I don't drink it."

"Aw, I knew you knew I would come. I knew it would be okay. You don't have to tell me directly, I get that it's hard for you," he says.

The blinking red countdown over his head hits 20:00. 19:59. 19:58.

We walk into the woods.

"Cheers," I say.

DC clinks his travel mug to mine and downs the drink.

"Seriously?" I say.

"You know me, I chug."

"I don't know why I waste the good scotch on you."

In the moonlight his grin is green.

"You love me," he says.

We set off. He wants to hold my hand. I let him for a moment because I know soon the path will be too narrow to continue.

"Aw," he says, when we have to split apart.

"Do you want me to carry the hatchet?" I ask.

But he's got it. I lead the way.

I get it. I was in love with a woman who turned me into someone new. She gave me books to read and podcasts to listen to, and I didn't think of it as indoctrination because the shit she gave me seemed to be right. I thought I was lucky. Someone so smart wanted to waste her time educating me. Why? I wasn't *that* young and hot. There was no explanation *but* love.

I changed my whole life for her. And you know what she did? She abandoned me. She got bored of me or finished her little project and left. I spent a lot of time trying to figure out if I was a radical blip in her normie life or if I was her last great radical love or if I inadvertently made radicalism seem ugly to her. I really perseverated on all of that for a long time after we broke up, trying to figure out who to become if I could get a chance to have her back.

"Ow," DC said, "my leg."

I smile.

"Did you bang it on a log?" I say.

"No?" he says.

He's cramping. How far are we from the grave?

He screams, a long, warbling cry, high enough to sound like a forest cat. Certainly no woman could ever love a person who made a noise like that. Certainly he knows that. Certainly he doesn't expect someone to go against their nature to do that. So certainly he, in a way, consented to all of this, by deluding himself.

His knees hit the ground first, then the rest of his body, heavy.

"You did great—we're pretty close," I say.

The shovel is only twenty feet away, I think. The hole I dug, less than that. Really, I have done well. I dosed him so perfectly he almost made it into his own grave, but not so close that he saw it coming.

He shudders and gurgles. I decide he is saying "Drink?"

"It's just strychnine, nothing fancy. Way more efficient than bribing a pharmacist, and easier than stabbing someone. You can just buy it online."

He reaches for his phone, but his muscles spasm too hard for him to get to it. He curls into a ball. I squat next to him to wait it out. What smells good? The trees? I kind of want to live forever in this forest.

X made me fall in love with her, then she reshaped me in her image. She just didn't have the guts to reshape herself. She could hate a rapist, but she could only see one way to punish him. Even if that way was 100 percent proven to fail, even if that way was a tool created by a broken system to make it look like justice existed without ever actually working, which she was able to twist to her advantage in every other facet of her fucking life.

Still, she couldn't help but blame me. I hadn't failed to do *anything*, but I had failed to do *everything*. That's what she wanted. She needed me to demolish myself against Meat Neck, batter myself to pieces against his protected hull. And then what? I would have been a pile of rubble. Instead, she left and made it impossible for me to love anyone but her, and she made the world look as poisonous as it really is. And in case that wasn't evil enough, she left a man to torture me in her stead and didn't care enough to do anything about it when I told her.

Or maybe I'm wrong, and love is just a form of hate, and watching someone suffer is just another great erotic activity. I guess I'm about to find out.

The clatter of breaking twigs stops. Gasping stops. Breath stops.

DC is dead. I reach down to close his eyes, but they're already closed.

My shoulders hurt and I haven't even gotten started. Not really. Why do I do that? Why do I constantly reset the clock? I get to the end of something and immediately rename it the beginning. Maybe it's part of my success. No, I know it is. It's been a busy three days, but here I am, standing on the precipice of a new task. Bury the body, clean my own, close up the guesthouse, hike out. Those are the next steps. When they are done, I'll be at the beginning of more.

I could give a talk on productivity. I could write a book. I could start a podcast. If podcasts weren't a magnet for friendless losers hopped up on parasocial relationships. *Focus on the moment. It's time to get going,* I tell myself. But I do not move. I stay next to the body a little longer.

Just this one last thing, I promise myself. Instead of getting started, I rest long enough for the forest sounds, which have been startled into quiet, to slowly return. The flutter of feathers, tiny footsteps over the twigs and soil, chewing, then more footsteps, hooting, a howl. I let my skin grow as cold as I can bear before I unfold from my crouch and begin again.

EPILOGUE

IT'S SUNNY. I chose that for X. The place I've rented is down a shady alley. The house is a square with a courtyard full of trees at the center. It's simple. I brought my things but barely use them. I am living in a swimsuit I bought in town. I found a flimsy blue tote bag in one of the drawers that I hang on a nail in the kitchen and use every day.

On the morning that the special four-part series *Killing Baby Hitler: Meat Neck and the Making of an American Folk Hero* goes live, I heat milk and start the moka pot. I slice fruit in half: papaya, avocado, mango. There are sweet buns. I wonder how long I can keep up the generous host facade. The first days I did it, days I knew she wouldn't come unless she deliberately ignored my request to wait, those days it felt like a treat for myself. That was six months ago.

Today the shine is back on. The air is moist and warm with a leafy smell below the coffee.

A month and a half ago Justice Bimbo announced a break from her podcast. *Finally, she's cutting my episodes*, I thought. I couldn't help myself; I wrote her.

"If there's anything you need to know," I typed, "I'm still here."

It took her more than a week to reply. That hurt.

"Going through some hard shit," she wrote back, "trying to focus on the work, though. Thanks for your offer, it helps."

Divorce, Reddit said. *Don't have to tell me, Reddit,* I told Reddit.

I considered emailing back to console her. A few years ago, I would have. But I let her be. It would have been more work than I wanted to do.

The public response to Meat Neck's death has been mixed. That scared me at first. I thought it might mean that X wouldn't come. But X won't let America's ambivalence interfere with what she knows is right. There are plenty of public fan letters, anyway. Ten-slide infographics with the history of Meat Neck's crimes, the truth as they know it about the assassination. There are memes. Triumphant, celebratory memes. No one knows who I am. I am depicted as a Black woman in short shorts. Sort of an Afro Lara Croft. I hope, if the truth is discovered, I'm not accused of racism just because I let that characterization go on. That makes me laugh. If that were the reason I were accused of racism, that would be hilarious. See. I'm having fun. It's a good day.

I have been enjoying a well-deserved break from all work except the simplest shopping and cooking. For a month I didn't even read a book! I just woke in the morning. Sat. Watched the ocean. Watched the trees. Watched the local birds.

There are cats here—a little gray-and-red kitten who must have some secret way into the courtyard. He lays splayed on his back with his eyes closed and runs away if you get close. There's a slinky white adult with half an ear missing who waits at my door in the mornings. I call her Oscar. So far, no one has found me aside from the cats. It's a pleasant place to recover.

At nine a.m. Central Time there's a new episode on Justice Bimbo's podcast feed. But it's only three minutes long. "Announcement," it's titled. My fear is that she is announcing she's quitting or that she will take even more time with this series or that she's calling it off. But it's none of these. She's just saying that premium listeners will be able to stream the entire series immediately, and a scripted message she says her attorney is making her read because the investigation is still ongoing. When I refresh the feed, the first episode is there, waiting.

If it's all available for premium listeners, then that's the end. I try to force a sigh of relief. I pull up Justice Bimbo's social media. She's posted a photo from this morning cheersing coffee mugs with her producer.

It's night when I hear the door open. I'm in bed but not yet asleep. I knew it would be tonight, I decide. I am not scared. I can smell her in the house, she smells like cold iron, sweat, and clean clothes. There is unzipping and zipping, zipping, unzipping. Bags. The tossing of clothes, the thudding of a backpack. I don't want to go out there, so I pretend I'm asleep, because if I were awake, I wouldn't be able to help myself.

Now she is in the room.

"I'm here," X says.

I am still fake asleep, so I say nothing. She gets into bed. Her body curves around mine. The first thing I feel is rage. But it subsides fast into desire. I roll over to her. Our mouths meet. There's no reason to be quiet, so I make her scream.

At five a.m., I slip out of bed for a run and a swim. I am lithe and strong. I am happy. And I'm all out of plan. I won't find out what comes next until I do it. This feels good. I have learned so much in the last year of work—about my resourcefulness, flexibility, charm. Then about my strength: emotional and physical.

The horizon is shades of blue. The first eight minutes of my run are always the same: excitement, then breathlessness, then exhaustion, then a burst of endorphins that can carry me far longer than I should go. I loop through the town, down to the beach, on a dirt path among low dunes, beside unfinished vacation homes. The air smells like rancid flowers. I predicted it would be surreal to have X here. Other times, I thought it would feel natural. Or I worried we would return to the bickering part of our relationship, near the end.

But now that she's here, it's different than any of the scenarios I imagined.

It is real but not natural. It's not fun but it's not stressful, either. No bickering yet. X is exactly as I remember. Her voice, the cadence she uses with me, her movements, her jokes with their unpredictable swerves into seriousness. I was afraid she'd want to stay up all night talking, but she didn't. We lasted an hour before she dozed off and I got up to brush my teeth. I'm the one who feels different. I am myself, but I am also a little foreign to myself.

For the decade since she left, my heart has been a heavy charm at the end of a chain. X held the charm with her always. Whenever I tried to love someone else, whenever I tried to weave curiosity and affection or desire and respect into something more, I couldn't. I didn't have access. It killed me. I wanted to move on so badly. I wanted love so much. *I will love someone so well*, I promised the universe, but no matter how hard I tried to cut the chain, I could not. I tried to bury the tether, just to see it wiggle back up to the surface every time I got close to someone else. A haunting little piece of hardware.

But even more than I wanted the chain to break, I wanted it to rip X back to me, and I did all kinds of things to make that happen. Liking her photos. Accidental nudes. Appearing (by text) as if by magic when she was sad. Anonymous postcards. *Tug back if you're still there.* She usually did. And she would yank on the chain without my prompting from time to time. But she never went as hard as I did. But how could she? Is there a bigger act of love than murder?

After four miles, I stop to stretch. My walk is a bounce as I strip down to my sports bra and underwear. I kneel in the water, dip my head under, swim out a bit farther, and float.

The danger is gone, my plan worked, she is here. X is in my house. My attention is not pouring constantly out of my body to find her. A part of me is not constantly reaching. I can chill the fuck out.

When I have regained my breath, I spot the rocky outcropping I always use as my turnaround point, drop my face in the water, and begin to swim. X is in my bed. I kick a little faster.

After my first month here, I started running every morning. I swim most days, if the current isn't dangerously strong. I'm not built for leisure. I guess I always knew that, but I really know now—in paradise with all the money in the world. I read books during the day. I take my ideas for swims with me. They multiply. They divide. They rise and disappear. A few weeks ago, I was on a swim and found Child Star in my head. He was wearing a swimsuit, lying on the beach.

"Nice place you got here," he said.

I said nothing. The swimsuit was a Speedo, which was distracting.

I had been in a foul mood that morning. I was anxious for X to arrive, or to tell me she was going to arrive, or to tell me she wasn't coming at all. The anxiety clustered in my crotch and my legs. I was trying to exercise it out, so it didn't turn to violence.

"You don't think so?" he said.

"Will I ever be done with X?" I asked him.

He answered right away, "Yes."

"When?" I insisted.

"Probably when you stop loving her," he said.

He should have been a therapist. He was my imaginary, slightly famous therapist. I don't know why it took something so simple to get through to me. The answer was a circle, the answer was redundant. You stop loving someone when you stop loving someone, which happens when you stop loving them because you stop loving them.

There's no way in! I would have thought it would make me feel hopeless but it made me feel good.

I leave the beach, just as the old men with their newspapers are packing up and families with young children are beginning to arrive. A child jumps out of the back of a pickup, followed by a dog, followed by a beach ball, followed by the kid who threw the beach ball.

On the way out of the lot, I see two men in suits and sunglasses. One waves. I stop walking. I nod back. Then a third man appears. A fourth.

And they all cross the street to a church just as a hearse rolls up.

I go home.

X is standing in the kitchen. My heart does not race. I am serene.

"Did you abandon me to work out?" She laughs. X used to work out.

"Learned it from you." I smile.

"Oh God, I wish I still had time for that," she says.

She is scraping eggs onto two plates. The kitchen is a wreck. She means her life is busy because she is important, adult, responsible. She means my life is vanity and hedonism. Her life is marriage. My life is two-hour beach workouts. She believes I live on vacation. How has she used every single dish in the kitchen to cook eggs?

"You have more time now," I say. My voice is even.

She laughs, she really laughs. My heart does a standing ovation for that laugh.

"You're right, I guess I do," she says.

I smile earnestly.

"I cooked, you wash?" she says. She is not really asking. I hand her the dish towel so she can dry. She folds it and hangs it up.

"I want to go to the beach," she says. But she doesn't leave. She sits down. She will watch me clean, then she will want me to go with her to the beach. Annoyance fizzles in the balls of my feet, my wrists. I crack my knuckles.

I was open to the possibility that X and I had changed in complementary ways, and that the death of Meat Neck and of the Stalker would balance each other out, and we would be able to love each other again. I thought that was a possibility. Well, I was open to thinking that was a possibility. But I'm not surprised with the way things have gone. Two deaths can't balance each other out if one person does both of them. If one person does absolutely everything—cleans up all the problems, sets up a new life for the other to move into, no strings attached. I did all the work, meanwhile X grew into a scold, and the worst kind of family man—the kind who leaves their wife for someone better.

None of this is a surprise. It's going the way I thought it would. This is the reality I created. The one magic wish I made was to be able to love again. Not to be able to love *her* again. Nothing is happening in the room. X is pinching her lips. She is picking at her cuticles. She is looking out the window. But it feels like I am moving, passing through this moment on the way to something else.

Automatically my mind goes to the Curator, who morphs into Blake Lively, who morphs into a grad student I met on the beach just a few days before X arrived. I think of the woman who sold me my swimsuit. I told her I was here to write a novel. She told me I was pretty, and said she hangs out at a bar down the beach with some locals. I think of my first girlfriend and then of my mother and I wonder what is happening with the guys.

How long will X have to be here before her marriage is irreparable? Maybe it already is. That's the final piece.

X is next to me, and, finally, the chain is slack, coiled between us like a sleeping creature. Turns out, the charm is not my heart after all. It's just a heavy steel ball. A fucking ball and chain. And I'm close enough for the first time to see that if I just reach over, I can undo the clasp myself.

"Can you close the window? It's too hot," X says.

A car alarm blares, a door slams. I hear the whir of a bike coasting by. My hand is on the crank. I breathe. I breathe again. I am looking for salt on the wind, or barbecue, or a flower I like, or a smell I recognize from long ago. None of those come. I close my eyes. Once I'm done here, I'll remember these smells instead: the tile cleaner I use for the kitchen floor, eggs, plumeria. The truth is, as soon as X entered this sweet little house, it felt like a place I was ready to leave.

"Hello?" she says. "Are you going to close it?"

She is brushing crumbs from the table to the floor. She is standing up.

I can do anything. I can go anywhere. I could get a car in town to the airport and leave today. Everything I need is in that little blue bag.

Does X even know that instead of judging you can just . . . do?

I close my eyes again and unclasp the chain. Who knows if X notices.

But I notice. I imagine us apart again and no urgent feelings arise. When I shift, the last bit of sand falls from my ankles to the floor and I swear I can hear it hit the ground. A shower of tiny musical crystals. X is just a person, any person. I don't know where my anger went but it is gone. I twist my ocean-damp hair up into a bun. My hands are deft. My shoulders are back. My neck is long and free of knots. My breath is steady. My heart is full. My love is a golden light. My love is a brilliant shining beacon gushing out of every dramatic step I've taken for her. My love pours over my friends and enemies alike. Love for my parents, my friends, for the guys, for strangers. I love dead Meat Neck and I love that I killed him. I love all the people of the world that I killed him for. And I feel turned on—by no one in particular. I'm alive. I'm curious. I'm young. I'm beautiful and hyper-articulate. Yes, now my love is a radiating light and it illuminates everyone but her.

ACKNOWLEDGMENTS

THANK YOU to Claudia Ballard, Fiona Baird, and the team at WME for taking a chance on me. Thank you to Margo Shickmanter, Allison Green, Amy Guay, Hana Handzija, and everyone at Avid Reader for making my work exponentially better. Thank you to Sophie Orme and my UK team at Bonnier. Thank you to all the other book biz people who helped to make me a better writer and to put this book in your hands: Harrison Demchick, David Varno, Sonya Cheuse, Torrey Peters, and Catherine Lacey. Thank you, Dan Novack!

I am so grateful to the many generous writers in my life. First among them is Temim Fruchter—thank you for workshopping names, menus, jokes, reveals, and gossip, and more than that thank you for your singing prose which always leaves me both wanting to read more and wanting to live more. Thank you to Murder Mystery Cuteb Clud, to the Acquitted Owl Retreat, Northern Spy Reading Series, and to Grit Group. Thank you to Caitlin MacBride, who is actually a painter (oil) not a writer. We learned how to be artists and moms together. I would absolutely not be here without you. Can't wait to see what we have to figure out next.

Most of this book was written on my phone in the grocery line, or in the front matter of novels in the daycare pickup line, in voice memos recorded between the visit from the nurse and the visit from the doctor, and in emails to myself whenever a colleague was running late. So none of this would have been possible without understanding (and truancy) from so many people, or without an army of people who gave notes and fed kids.

Thank you to Amanda, Alyx, Khalid, Sylvana, Pau, Allison, Lee, Adam, Adam, Emma, Emma, Caitlin, Caitlin, Laura, Laura, Lauren, Lauren, Molly, Molly, Jen, Jen, Jessica, Jessica, Jess, Ana, Ginny, Dick, Anouk, Mina, Skylar, and Lilly. Thank you to Megan, Georgia, Elizabeth, Blythe, Jack, Patty, Akiya, Julia, Maddie, Miyagi, Toni, Peggy, Will, Daye, Max, Tahira, Emily, Emmet, Damien, Zan, Raechel, Sofia, Wazina, Daisy, Quinn, Ryan, CJ, KC, KT, Erin, Gareth, Jon, Rahne, and Dr. V. Thank you to Bondo for just one more sentence. And to my children for the just three more sentences after that.

Thank you to all my teachers at Mapleton Elementary, Casey Middle School, and Boulder High—especially Kenneth Nova for the "instead of said" list, Tiff Boyd for everything, Sra. Harvey, Sra. Diaz, Ms. Fiori, Mr. Jewel, Jean and Tony McGinnis, Eleni Arapkiles, and Scott Partridge. To Janet and Jerome. To the Boulder Public Library. To Hog Island Audubon Camp. To the rail trails of the Hudson Valley, especially the ones with bats.

Thank you to all my sisters: of blood or of contract or of affinity or in Christ.

But above all thank you to Kristof Wickman—artist, fabricator, dad, my heart. Thank you for passing the work back and forth with me. Is it labor or is it pleasure? What a dream.

ABOUT THE AUTHOR

REBECCA NOVACK grew up in Colorado. She has a master's in theological studies from Harvard Divinity School and lives in New York.